Also by Jennae Vale

The Thistle & Hive Series
A Bridge Through Time - Book 1
A Thistle Beyond Time - Book 2
Separated By Time - Book 3
A Matter of Time - Book 4

The Mackalls of Dunnet Head
Her Trusted Highlander

A HIGHLANDER IN Vegas

JENNAE VALE

For my family and friends, who've been my support throughout this process. And to you, dear reader. Without your support and encouragement this would not be possible.

CHAPTER 1

BRAEDEN MACDONALD WAS anything but a coward. He'd never run from a fight in the entirety of his thirty years on this earth. That is, not until this very day. The fact that death shadowed him as he ran only made him run faster and faster still. Sweat dripped in long rivulets from his body despite the frigid temperatures on this cursed February day and steam escaped his nostrils and mouth in dragon like bursts as he raced. Charging headlong through the trees and brambles, which were thickly covered in a fresh blanket of snow, desperation was his only companion. Fear for his own life was not what made him run. He'd come to grips with the fact that by the end of this day he'd be dead, as would so many others. All around him gunshots rang out followed by the cries of those falling and dying as this unexpected massacre rained down upon them, perpetrated by those who would call themselves guests of Clan MacDonald. Anger fueled his legs and kept him going when exhaustion would have had him give up. He had to warn the others. It was all he could think to do. These people, his family, his clan must be saved somehow. Even as he repeated this over and over to himself, he knew it to be a futile effort.

Robert Campbell and a troop of soldiers had been billeted with the MacDonald's of Glencoe. Alistair Maclain, as chief of The MacDonalds, welcomed them and treated them as honored guests. Little did he know that his reward for such hospitality was to be shot dead as he rose from his bed on the morning of this fateful day. The orders were to kill every MacDonald under the age of seventy and so they were cut down where they stood or as they tried to run to safety. Braeden MacDonald knew the futility of standing his ground and fighting. He would be dead in no time at all. Instead he had chosen to run to the homes of his fellow clansmen, to warn them of the danger that was headed in their direction. The acrid smell of smoke stung his nose and eyes as he realized that there was nary a home left standing and there was no one remaining for him to warn. As he ran, his grandmother's words rang in his ears.

"Braeden, you must escape this slaughter," Esther MacDonald cried as she pressed something into the palm of his hand.

"Grannie, I must warn the others." All around him the sounds of gunfire and chaos filled the air. "I cannae think of myself at a time like this." He looked down at the object his grandmother had given him. "What's this?"

Esther MacDonald grasped Braeden's chin in what he assumed was an effort to make him listen to her, to look into her eyes and understand what she was telling him. "It's a pocket watch, Braeden. It has magical powers. If ye find yerself unable to escape, all ye need do is hold it to yer heart, think of yer Ma and wish to go to the meadows." Her eyes searched his face. Her concern for him was evident, but Braeden refused to save himself at the expense of other lives being lost to these damn Campbells. The fear and commotion must have made his grandmother lose her mind. How could a pocket watch be magical? "Please. Please. Promise me that if ye find yerself in danger, ye'll do as I've told ye."

Braeden glanced at the watch. He'd never seen it before, but he had no time to examine it now. Shouts were heard coming their way. "I promise, Grannie." He put the pocket watch in his sporran and grabbed her by the arm. "We must hurry. They'll be on us in the blink of an eye."

"Dinnae worry for me, Braeden. I will escape. They have no interest in an old woman like me. 'Tis ye they're after." Esther sat down on the side of the path, tears shining in her eyes and streaming down her cheeks. "Go, Braeden. God be with ye."

"I love ye, Grannie. I'll be back for ye." Braeden hesitated, but knowing she was right he reluctantly left her and ran into the woods. He sped to the next cottage down the path with the intent of warning those who called it home, but as he approached, he could see he was too late. The dead bodies of those who'd resided there lay still where they'd fallen as they'd obviously tried to run from their attackers, who then set their home ablaze. It was now not much more than a smoldering pile of ashes. Braeden felt the bile rising in his throat and his anger flamed at the injustice of it all. This land he'd called home since he was a bairn, was now destroyed by the stench of death and blood coming from every direction. He was so consumed by the sight in front of him that he didn't hear the Campbells as they approached, until it was too late. He was surrounded by them. As they laughed and aimed their pistols at him, Braeden realized he wasn't going to make it out of this alive. He reached into his sporran for the pocket watch and did as his Grannie had told him. He didn't remember his Ma, but he thought of her anyway and imagined what she might have looked like. He could see her there in his mind's eye, a much younger version of his beloved Grannie. "I wish to go to the meadows," he managed to choke the words from his throat, and then a shot rang out. He saw it all in slow motion, watching it as if he were already outside of his body. He felt nothing as the images before his eyes blurred and he thought to himself that dying wasn't so bad after all.

For a moment the men surrounding him looked baffled, and then they lunged for him just as Braeden felt himself blacking out, surrounded by silence and darkness.

CHAPTER 2

THE GRAND OPENING of The Albannach Resort Hotel and Casino saw throngs of people passing through the doors of the elaborate Scottish castle situated on Las Vegas Boulevard. It was the newest hotel on the Strip and was built to resemble an authentic seventeenth-century castle, but with all the modern conveniences that attracted visitors to Sin City. John McTavish, the owner, and his daughter Tessa McTavish had their hands full greeting visitors and making sure that everything was running smoothly. The registration desk had a line that wove its way through a zigzag maze of people and luggage before stopping in front of the twenty registration clerks on duty. Gamblers and sightseers wanting to be among the first to experience what the casino had to offer, filled the lobby of The Albannach to overflowing. It seemed that every man, woman and child in the state of Nevada was present and many stood with mouths agape as they entered, admiring the grand beauty found in every detail, large and small.

If it wasn't for the slot machines and gaming tables, the experience of being in a real seventeenth-century Scottish castle would have visitors believing they'd been transported back in time to a place where Scottish lairds and ladies resided. This was especially true when Trevor McDaniels and Livia Hidalgo made their way through the crowds, greeting their guests, stopping for photos and chatting with visitors. While the building was constructed to meet all the modern safety requirements of the twenty-first century, the facade of the building created the magic. Limestone walls had been carefully carved into large blocks of stone stacked one atop the other. Authentic fireplaces were placed here and there around the casino floor. John had enlisted the help of a friend in the Magick and Sorcery community to create a very real looking fire in each, without the use of actual flames, wood or heat. The effect was one that mesmerized the visitors, who stood around them in awe of what they were seeing.

"Is that fire real?" A teenage boy in all his surly glory was about to put his hand in to find out.

"Don't touch that. You'll get burned," his mother said, slapping his hand away from the fireplace.

"It's not even hot." His hand darted towards the flames once again. This time his mother wasn't quick enough to stop him as he snaked his hand directly into the fire. Pulling it back out he gaped at it with a look of awe on his face.

"Oh no, are you okay? Did you burn yourself?" She seemed as if she might cry at her son's predicament.

Tessa thought it would be a good idea to intervene at this point. "It's not a real fire," she assured the mother.

"Not real? Then how…?" She wore a baffled expression.

"Just a bit of Las Vegas magic." Tessa smiled and continued on her way, keeping stride with John all the way.

"Dad, I'm amazed at the wonderful job the Magick and Sorcery Society did." Tessa was marveling at the way the lighting, which was once again reminiscent of the past, had also been magically spelled to appear as candles, while emanating more than enough light for the patrons to see everything.

"Well, I didn't ask Niall for the Society's help. He'd never have agreed. The man doesn't like me. I don't know what I ever did to him, but even though he's very pleasant when we meet, I can feel his disdain for me whenever he's close."

"I thought the Society did all this." She pulled her father out of the way of a couple so enthralled with what they were seeing that they almost collided with John.

"I called Bobby Noonan for help. He's a far greater sorcerer than Niall, but he'll have nothing to do with him anymore. He's working in a small casino off the strip."

"Really, why?"

"Niall wanted him to focus more on the dark arts and Bobby refused. He was banned from the Society and black-listed from working at any of the larger venues here in town."

"That's too bad. Bobby's such a nice man and he did an unbelievable job here at the casino."

A tall, dark haired man approached them with his hand extended. "Are you John McTavish?"

"I am." John looked quizzically at the man.

"I'm Rhys Adamson. I just wanted to congratulate you on the grand opening and let you know that my wife and I can't believe how beautiful everything is. This is almost as good as actually going to Scotland and visiting an old castle."

"I'm happy to hear it," John said. "This is my daughter, Tessa. If you need anything at all, please don't hesitate to ask. We aim to please."

"You sure do. Everything is spectacular. The guest room doors are so beautiful. So far I haven't seen any two that are alike. I feel like I've stepped into another century. We will definitely be coming back." He shook both their hands before excitedly making his way to the Black Jack tables.

John and Tessa watched him as he walked away. Tessa had chosen each of the hand-crafted wooden doors, trimmed with ornate metal work that led to the rooms. The idea was to make each room distinctive in any way possible so the guests felt like royalty. Everything from the beds to the en suites, which were constructed to resemble an intimate stone grotto, were custom designed for each room. So far the guests couldn't be happier with the experiences available to them at The Albannach.

The hotel staff had been carefully chosen and trained on the proper way to handle their guests. They wore authentic Scottish attire that had been adjusted to accommodate what had come to be expected by all those who journeyed to Vegas for a carefree and fun experience. The lasses wore tiny versions of the McTavish plaid in the form of a quasi kilt and an off-the-shoulder white blouse. The family crest was crafted into a pewter name pin, which adorned each of them. The lads who made up the security staff were dressed in authentic looking seventeenth-century kilts, and the gaming crew wore more modern day versions of the traditional kilts and jackets for practical reasons.

"Everything seems to be going smoothly," John McTavish observed as he eyed the casino floor.

"This is so exciting!" Tessa couldn't imagine how her father remained so calm about everything.

"Yes. That it is, my dear. That it is." John began walking towards the cashier's booth and Tessa followed along behind. Lines of people were waiting to cash in their chips and armed security guards stood by the elaborate gate that led into the inner sanctum, behind the cashiers. Tessa was particularly proud of the gate. She'd designed it and had it made at a local metal shop. It was set into an arched limestone wall. The gate itself was a beautifully polished brass showing The Celtic Tree of Life, whose gnarled roots were symbolic of the entrance to The Otherworld. The cashiers sat behind grates of a similar style, dressing the bulletproof glass at each station meant to protect the cashiers from harm if someone made the mistake of trying to rob them. Security cameras were set up throughout the casino and on each of the hotel floors. No one went unseen at The Albannach. The cameras were not meant to invade anyone's privacy, but safety and security were paramount in the casino business and John wanted his guests to feel a sense of ease when they were at his hotel. The idea was to be vigilant without being obtrusive.

John had worked his way up the ranks at some of the best casinos on the strip. It wasn't that he needed to work. On the contrary, the McTavish fortune was well known in Las Vegas. At an early age, he decided that in order to be the best casino owner possible it was in his best interest to learn all of the jobs associated with running a successful venture like The Albannach, and then perfecting them.

"Is everything going smoothly," John asked Margaret Camden, the woman in charge of the cashiers.

"Yes, sir. No problems at all. I'd say that's pretty good for an opening day." Margaret smiled proudly at her boss.

"Congratulations, Margaret! Keep up the good work." John and Tessa stood watching the cashiers and customers for a few moments before moving back onto the casino floor. They passed the gaming tables where everyone appeared to be happily having a good time and then on to the banks of slot machines. Again, everything was running smoothly. They had already checked in on the bars and restaurants and spoke with the events coordinator about upcoming weddings, conferences and special happenings. Tessa would be working closely with the events coordinator, as she was the hotel wedding planner. Things couldn't be going any better.

"I'm going to my office, Tessa. Keep an eye on things on the floor, would you?" John turned to her and with a fatherly gleam in his eyes, pinched her cheek, much as he'd done since she was a tiny little girl. Tessa wrinkled her nose in feigned irritation, but secretly she found it very sweet.

"Of course, Dad. I'd be happy to." Tessa watched her father as he made his way through the crowds, stopping briefly to speak with someone she didn't recognize. Her father seemed quite agitated about something and she was just about to go see what was going on when the man swiftly turned and left. As she observed, John disappeared into the crowd and Tessa headed for the Las Vegas Boulevard entrance to see that everyone was being greeted properly. She made a mental note to ask her father what that was all about when she saw him later.

There were always more characters to be found in Las Vegas than anywhere else in the world as far as she could tell. The number of outlandish sights she saw on a daily basis was sometimes hard to fathom.

She'd gotten quite used to it over the years, but for people visiting the Strip for the first time, or even those returning, it could be quite the show. As she passed one of the casino bars, she spotted a case in point. A shirtless man, dressed in a kilt, was standing atop the bar drunkenly singing at the top of his lungs. "O you take the low road and I'll take the high road and I'll be in Scotland afore ye. For me and my true love will ne-er meet again on the bonnie, bonnie banks of Loch Lomond."

Before he could start the second verse, Tessa moved to stand by the bar. The bartender had motioned to her that security had been called, so she knew they'd be on their way. For now, her only thought was to get him off the bar before he fell. "I think you've got the words a little mixed up. It should be 'you take the high road and I'll take the low road."

"Isn't that what I said?"

"No. It wasn't." Tessa sat on a bar stool and continued engaging him in conversation for a few moments before standing again and holding out a hand to him as he swayed back and forth. "Why don't you come down from there?"

"If that means I get to hold your hand, then I'll gladly come down." He gave her his hand and sitting down on the bar, scooted to the edge and off, landing on the floor in a heap, his kilt askew, showing much more than Tessa or anyone else at the bar wanted to see.

"Are you okay?" Tessa asked as she helped him up.

"Yes, ma'am. I'm perfectly fine." His eyes were practically crossed at this point.

"Are you staying here at the hotel?"

"I am. Do you want my room number?" He ogled Tessa, a slow smile forming on his lips, which made her feel quite uncomfortable.

"I do." The smell of alcohol on his breath was intense. The closer he got to her, the queasier she felt. Tessa nonchalantly covered her nose with her hand.

"I'm in room 2016. Like this year." He was slurring his words badly and was now swaying on his feet. "You gonna come see me later?" The comically hopeful way he asked caused Tessa to laugh, which she tried to cover with a cough. "Hey, are you laughing at me?" He was about to fall again when security arrived and took over.

"He's staying in room 2016. Can you see to it that he gets back there safely and have Doctor Simons check in on him? He's had much too much to drink."

The security team knew exactly what to do. They led the drunken man to the elevators. He serenaded them the whole way there and Tessa couldn't help but chuckle. "Disinfect that bar top, would you please, Zach." Tessa wrinkled her nose at him.

"I'm a step ahead of you boss. I did it while you were handling our friend," Zach smiled and winked at Tessa.

"Oh, and Zach, one more thing. We don't want patrons getting that inebriated. He should not have gotten to that point."

"I called security as soon as he showed up and I refused to serve him. Next thing I knew he climbed up on the bar and started singing." Zach leaned on the bar as he spoke. "You don't need to worry about me. I was paying close attention during training."

"I'm sure you were. I just had to be sure it wasn't you who got him that drunk." Tessa smiled warmly at Zach who happily returned to his adoring female audience. He flipped and juggled a few bottles, much to their delight, and continued filling drink orders. He was an adorable guy and the ladies loved him. He kept the bar filled with them from morning till night during their soft opening of the prior week, and it appeared now that the hotel was officially open, it was going to continue. Tessa stood back and watched him work his magic. The ladies had crowded around him, each vying for his attention. It appeared they were relieved that the crooning Scotsman had left and they had Zach all to themselves again.

IF THE GOAL was to seamlessly transport people from twenty-first-century Las Vegas to seventeenth-century Scotland, from the looks on the faces of those entering the casino, she'd say they were very successful.

"How's everything going, Livia?" Tessa found the laird and his lady during a brief moment of quiet.

"This is amazing! I can't believe how many people have stopped to take photos." Livia was smiling brightly at Tessa and then turned her radiant smile on Trevor. "Wouldn't you agree, Trevor?"

"Unbelievable!" Trevor chucked his lady under the chin. "It doesn't hurt that I've got the most beautiful woman in all of Las Vegas playing the part of my wife. People are eating it up."

Tessa noted that the two had become quite close over the last few days of preparation and she hoped it wouldn't all end in disaster if they tired of each other's company. That wouldn't be good for them or for the casino. She didn't want to think that way though. Instead, she'd believe that if there was anything going on between the two of them that it would be a good thing and she was happy for them. Still, the way they looked at each other—Tessa wished her fiancé would look at her that way. She'd only been engaged a short time, but she didn't feel as excited as she'd expected she would about getting that ring, and if she really thought about it, Danny didn't seem as over the moon as she'd thought he would either. In reality, she was quite surprised by his proposal and even more surprised that she'd accepted. The whole evening had been a blur to her, like she'd been under some crazy spell and as soon as she was alone in her room she found herself wondering whether she'd made a mistake by saying yes. They hadn't really been dating that long and the more she examined her feelings, the more she didn't want to think about it. She chalked it up to all the excitement of the casino opening overwhelming everything else in her life. Now that they were celebrating their Grand Opening, Tessa hoped she could devote more time to her personal life and to Danny.

"Is everything alright, Tessa?" Livia placed a gentle hand on Tessa's arm. Tessa guessed that she was wearing her heart on her sleeve, as she was prone to do.

"Things couldn't be better." She noted that Livia and Trevor exchanged questioning glances before bidding her goodbye and wandering into the crowd that had just made their way through the door.

Putting on his best Scottish accent, Trevor called out to the crowd. "Welcome to ye! We're pleased to have ye here in our home."

Tessa couldn't help but smile. Trevor was taking his job as laird of the castle very seriously. She gazed at the crowds entering the casino, her eyes searching for the man her father told her was coming in to interview for the job as head of security. John had asked her to keep an eye out for him. She had absolutely no idea what he looked like, but she'd decided to stay by the entrance and see if she could spot him as he entered.

CHAPTER 3

THE INCREDIBLE HEAT beating down on Braeden as he opened his eyes was almost unbearable. He'd never felt heat like it before. He blinked a few times to adjust his eyes to the bright light and as he became more aware of his surroundings, he had a moment of panic. *Where am I? Who are all these people?* The loud noises that reached his ears were constant and came from all directions. Feeling the need to escape the incredible noise, odd smells and throngs of people, Braeden grasped the watch to his chest once more. Closing his eyes, he thought again of his mother, as his Grannie had instructed, and wished with all his might to be taken to the meadows. He waited a moment or two before opening his eyes again, but much to his dismay, when he did he noted that nothing had happened. He remained, as he had been, feet firmly planted in this strange place, unsure of what to do next and fearing that he may burst into flames at any moment.

There were certainly no meadows that he could see. Instead, crowds of oddly clothed people surrounded him. The streets were filled with unusual carriages transporting people to who knows where and, strangest of all, he could see no horses pulling those bizarre coaches. The thought occurred to him that perhaps he was dead, maybe even a ghost, standing here among the living.

"Am I dead?" He spoke the words loudly, startling those closest to him on the street who turned to stare, and then laughing turned away. *They can see me and hear me. Surely that's a good sign. Mayhap they're dead as well.* The last things that he remembered were the advancing Campbells and the sound of a gunshot. He had been quite sure he'd meet his end there at their hands and it was possible that he had, although he didn't recall feeling any pain and he didn't remember anything that had happened after he made the wish on his pocket watch.

The crowds closed in around him and before he knew what was

happening he felt himself being bumped and jostled in the direction of a large castle. He struggled to stand his ground, but to no avail. It was as if he had no will of his own as he was drawn along with the crowds, closer and closer to the castle doors. Strange thoughts assailed his brain. Was he in heaven… or hell? The uncomfortable heat and noise had him believing it was the latter, but a moment later he was shoved through a rotating door into the very cool interior of the castle. Were there castles in heaven? He stood wide-eyed and unsure of where to go, something that was foreign to him. Braeden had always been very sure of himself, but the wonder of all he saw stripped him of his confidence. He was happy to be away from the oppressive heat, but the crowds and noise still surrounded him, making it difficult to think.

"You must be here for the security job." A soft, feminine voice startled him back to reality. A beautiful lass with flaxen hair stood before him. "I like your attention to detail," she said as she waved a hand in front of him. He was sure he couldn't help the dumbfounded expression on his face. "Nice costume, but if you plan on working here, you'll need the McTavish plaid. Follow me." She began to walk away and Braeden felt compelled to follow.

"Am I in heaven?" he asked, gaping at every extraordinary thing they passed. The lass gave him an appraising look back over her shoulder, before answering.

"Funny. For some people it's heaven and for others it's definitely hell."

So heaven and hell were in the same place. He would never have guessed it. "Are ye an angel?"

"If you're trying to score points with me, flattery will get you nowhere." The lass seemed to be getting irritated with him, but why? And what exactly did she mean 'scoring points.'

"I'm sorry, lass. 'Tis only that I'm new here and I'm unfamiliar with yer customs. If this is heaven, then it would make sense that ye be an angel." He tipped his head, furrowing his brow in question.

"Right. Have you just arrived from Scotland?" She continued walking and Braeden had to admit he enjoyed the way she moved in her unusual clothing and shoes. Her long blonde locks cascaded halfway down her back. She turned to look at him and he was taken aback by her beautiful sapphire eyes.

"Aye. I have. Are there those who are here from other places?" He glanced quickly around at the others moving about the castle.

The lass sighed. "Of course. There are people here from all over the world." She nodded and smiled at people as they passed. She must be a woman of some importance here, as the others seemed to show her much deference and appeared eager for her to notice them.

"I see." He didn't really see, but he could tell she was losing patience with him. "Where are we going?"

"I'm taking you to see my father. He'll want to meet you."

Her father? If they were in heaven, then that would mean… "Would that be our heavenly father?"

Tessa snickered at his question. "Some people around here might think that, but he doesn't like being thought of that way. He wants to be considered another employee like the rest of us."

"Employee?" So many confusing words entering his already addled brain.

"I know. It's kind of crazy. He is the boss after all and he owns this place, but he knows what it's like to work at every single job in the casino and he empathizes with those who work here. They love him for it. You'll see."

Braeden's head was spinning. He really had no idea what was going on, but he assumed this boss would tell him.

They came to a wall of doors and the lass stopped and nodded to others who were waiting. "I'm sorry, I forgot to introduce myself. I'm Tessa McTavish." She held out her hand to him, and he looked at it and then into her lovely face. She smiled reassuringly and he took her hand, bringing it to his lips.

"I be Braeden MacDonald. I'm pleased to make yer acquaintance." He released her hand and she snatched it back, appearing somewhat red in the face and flustered.

The doors slid open and Tessa walked into a very small room. Braeden followed and jumped when the doors closed behind him. He didn't like being out of his element and he certainly didn't want Tessa to think him frightened or unsure of himself. She hadn't seemed to notice. He stood with his back to the closed doors and Tessa stood facing him. Lifting a single eyebrow in apparent disbelief, she twirled her finger in the air, confusing him even further when she then ignored him, looking just above his head. He spun in place and gazed upwards, but saw nothing. Was he doing something wrong? Before he could ask her, the doors slid open again and she brushed past him as she left. He followed and was surprised to be in an entirely different place than when he'd first entered the wee space. Why had they gone in there? He had so many questions. He'd have to ask the boss when he met him. He didn't wish to antagonize the angelic lass anymore than he already had.

Tessa was heading down a long passageway with doors interspersed along the walls. At the very end was another beautiful woman, this one a red-head, seated behind a table.

"Kelly, can you tell my father that the man is here for the security position he has open."

"Sure." Kelly poked at something on the table and a male voice spoke from out of nowhere.

"Yes."

"Tessa's here with the man applying for the security position."

"Fine. Send them in."

Braeden searched high and low with his eyes trying to see where the voice was coming from. Was the man invisible? Kelly poked at something else on the desk and a set of double doors opened into another room.

Tessa passed through them and Braeden followed. The room was large and had soaring windows that looked out on the unfamiliar place in which he found himself. Braeden couldn't understand how he'd gone from the bottom floor of this strange castle to the very top without climbing any stairs. They were up so high. This really must be heaven.

The man stood and held out his hand and introduced himself. "John McTavish."

"Braeden MacDonald." Braeden grasped his hand and gazed questioningly into the man's eyes. So he wasn't God, unless, of course, God went by the name John McTavish.

"I've been expecting you. Please have a seat." John motioned to a most comfortable-looking chair and then sat down opposite him. "Tessa, you can leave us, but don't go too far. I'd like you to show Braeden around should I choose to hire him."

"I'll be right outside." Tessa walked out of the room and Braeden followed her with his eyes.

"She's a beauty, isn't she?" John's question seemed genuine, but Braeden was surely not going to speak his mind about the man's daughter.

"Aye," was all he could think to say.

"Braeden, I'm in need of someone to fill a security position. Do you think you could do that for me?"

"Aye."

"You're a man of few words. I like that. This job may not be as easy as it would seem." John paused and Braeden wondered if he should say something, but thought another aye would not be called for.

"I need someone to keep an eye on Tessa. To be her bodyguard." In Braeden's estimation, John McTavish was sizing him up.

"Is she in danger, sir?" Who could possibly wish harm upon the lovely angel? Braeden still thought he might be in heaven and if so, then Tessa was surely the most beautiful of angels. Perhaps John was the one he'd heard about from the priests, the one who guarded the gates of heaven and questioned all those who wished to enter.

"I believe she is. Do you think you have the proper qualifications to take on that job?" John tipped his head and cocked an eyebrow.

"Aye. I do." Braeden felt sure he could protect the lass without issue.

"Explain."

After a momentary pause, where Braeden wondered what exactly he was doing here, he answered, proudly sitting taller and puffing out his chest. "I'm a warrior sir. I've trained since I was a wee one to fight for the honor of my clan. I'm an expert with sword and dirk, good with me fists. I willnae let anyone harm Tessa." He said this with confidence, because he knew it was the truth.

"Good. That's what I wanted to hear." John's gaze never left Braeden's face.

"Ye said ye were expecting me. How did ye ken I was coming?" He needed some answers and he hoped this John McTavish, whoever he was, could give them to him.

"Where are you from, Braeden?"

"Scotland, sir." Braeden felt simple answers to be the best under the circumstances. He didn't wish to say too much before he had all the answers he sought.

"I know that," chuckled John. "I want details. I want to know where you've come from, who your family is, why you're here."

Braeden felt he had no choice but to answer truthfully. He was going to have to trust John McTavish, especially if he wished to continue his journey to the meadows. "I'm from Clan MacDonald, Glencoe, Scotland. We were under attack from the Campbells." Memories flooded his brain with images he'd never forget. The sights, sounds and smells were overwhelming, but for now he had no choice other than to bear it. Through clenched teeth, he managed to choke out the rest of it. "I tried to warn the others, but I was too late. My Grannie gave me a special pocket watch and told me it would take me to the meadows." His shoulders sagged as a deep sadness covered him in a blanket of regret. "It didnae work fer I've come here instead."

John laughed and shook his head. "This is the meadows lad. It's Las Vegas the Spanish word for the meadows. Your Grannie was right in what she told you." John stood and began pacing back and forth. "You were in the Glencoe Massacre." He stopped in front of Braeden, eyeing him with what appeared to be a mix of disbelief and amazement. "I can't believe it worked. I didn't believe him when he told me, but here you are in the flesh."

Braeden sat completely still. He shouldn't be surprised at all that this man knew where he'd come from. If he were truly God, or his right hand man, then he knew all. "Am I in heaven, sir?"

John laughed heartily again. "I suppose it may seem that way to you, but no. Yer only in Las Vegas."

"My head feels addled. I'm not sure what's happening to me. If I'm not in heaven, then I'm not dead?"

"No. You're quite alive. I'm amazed that it worked." John shook his head in apparent disbelief.

"What worked, sir?" Braeden had hoped for answers, but with every question he asked, he became more and more confused.

"Call me John, please. Let me explain. You have a pocket watch." It was more of a statement than a question.

"Aye." Braeden reached into his sporran and removed the watch. He clutched it in his hand, as it was the only thing that seemed real to him in this moment.

"And how did you get it?" John McTavish was grinning from ear to ear and Braeden thought he might be about to break into laughter again.

"'Twas given to me."

"Just as I thought. The watch you hold in your hands once belonged to an old friend."

Braeden controlled his reaction to this new information.

"So, you were given the watch by…" John was making him nervous with the intensity of his stare.

"Me Grannie gave it to me, sir." Braeden feared the watch would be taken from him and he clutched it more tightly in his hands.

"Do you know where she got it?"

"Nae. I dinnae."

"Don't worry, Braeden. We'll figure this out. The watch has special properties, lad. My understanding is that it was only to be used in times of danger. If the person who gave the watch to your Grannie was my old friend, he must have instructed her to give you the watch and tell you to wish to go to the meadows. You were apparently in danger, so she gave it to you and here you are." He smiled triumphantly at Braeden.

"I dinnae ken." This John McTavish must think him quite thick.

"You've travelled through time. You're in the future, lad. The year 2016 to be exact. I imagine you must be full of questions."

Braeden clamped his mouth shut in an effort to appear unaffected by what he was hearing. He felt as if the ground had been yanked from beneath his feet for the second time this day. He never liked to appear vulnerable, so it was vitally important that he keep the shock he felt from showing on his face, replacing it with one he used to frighten his enemies. John was still speaking excitedly to him, not seeming at all affected by his fierce glare.

"This is amazing. Don't worry. I'll be sure you're well taken care of and in return ye'll look after Tessa."

He had more questions this one day than he'd had his entire life. "Ye said she was in danger. Is someone trying to harm her?"

"I believe her fiancé, Danny Madden, is using her to get to me. As a matter of fact, I'm quite sure he cast a spell on her to get her to say yes to his marriage proposal. I don't believe she would have agreed otherwise. There is another involved who would love nothing more than to see me fail and he wants that pocket watch most of all. He tried to steal it from my friend many years ago."

"Why would he want this if he's already here?" Braeden had always thought himself quite clever, but at this moment he felt the exact opposite. He felt like a daft idjit, barely able to understand what was taking place around him.

"Good point, but you see the watch has the ability to not only transport you through time—any time, past, present or future—but it also has the ability to make time stand still. There is evil magic afoot here and the watch, in the wrong hands, would be a disaster. May I?" John pointed to the watch in Braeden's hands.

Handing the watch to John, he felt a twinge of concern. What if he didn't give it back? What would he do then?

John examined the watch, handling it with obvious care. "Do you believe in magic, Braeden?"

Braeden remained silent, not sure how to respond to John's question. He certainly couldn't argue that there was no such thing as magic. He'd seen first hand that there was. Why would he question any of this?

John didn't wait for an answer. He held the watch up in front of him. "The problem for us, Braeden, is that just as I knew you had arrived, or more precisely that the watch had arrived, my enemies knew you were here as well. You see, the watch announced its presence as soon as it entered this century."

"How do they know me?"

"I'm sorry. I'm not doing a very good job of explaining this to you. It's not that they know you, but they do know that the watch is here and that someone brought it back and has it in their possession. They know because the watch has been here before. My friend Ian left with it, and knowing the legend of the watch, they also know that he would have either brought it back himself or given it to his firstborn son. The fact that they don't know who you are works in our favor for now."

John handed the watch back to a startled Braeden who glanced down at it as it lay in his hands. "You knew my father? He was here?"

"I did and he was."

So many questions popped into his head, but it seemed all he could do was look at the watch. He hadn't taken the time to examine it too closely when his Grannie had given it to him. There'd been no time. Now he could see that it was a very beautiful timepiece. The case was made of gold and silver and encrusted with precious gems set in the pattern of a beautiful bird. It was quite solid and had weight to it. Braeden moved to open the case, but John held up a hand.

"Don't, please. The watch has great power as I've said and opening the case could not only unleash it but it would stop time and possibly give more information to my enemies about where to find it." John moved to hover over Braeden's shoulder. "It is best kept with you at all times. Never let it out of your sight."

"Who is this man who wishes to have possession of my watch?" Braeden was curious to know more, after all it was his watch and he was not willing to give it up to anyone, especially now that he knew it had come to him from his father. He wondered why his Grannie had kept this information from him. His father had been back and yet he hadn't seen him. Why? His thoughts were interrupted as John began speaking.

"There is a group here in Las Vegas. They are known as The Las Vegas Society of Magick and Sorcery. They are led by a man named Niall Campbell, and are a group of very dangerous men who are proficient in the dark arts. Niall Campbell wishes to possess the watch because if he has it and opens it, the Society will have the ability to make time stand still, which would then give them access to all the money and power they could ever want."

"Campbell!" The name had Braeden seeing red. "No Campbell shall ever possess this watch. Show me where he is and I'll gladly kill him for ye." Thoughts of his clansmen came to mind. Their dead bodies strewn across MacDonald lands. No Campbell would ever be safe from Braeden. He would avenge the MacDonald deaths, no matter what it took.

"I can see you're quite angry. The Glencoe Massacre, as it is called in today's history books, happened in 1692, and while it's still fresh in your mind, it occurred over 300 years ago. In today's world you can't simply go around killing Campbells."

Braeden narrowed his eyes and stared menacingly at John. "If I'm not here to avenge the deaths of my clan, then why am I here?" He asked this with a low, dangerous growl.

"Your Grannie knew you needed to be saved to carry on the family line. Your arrival here was a blessing, because you're needed, lad. I need you. Tessa needs you and the city of Las Vegas needs you." John patted his shoulder, leaving his hand there for a moment as Braeden's breathing returned to normal and his posture became less rigid.

"My coming here is a good thing?" Back to normal once again, or as close to normal as anyone could be under these circumstances, he awaited John's answer.

"Yes. I'd say it is. It's good because you needed to escape the Campbells or you would otherwise be dead. It's also good because I need your help and I believe you to be a man I can trust. I can see by the look on your face you wonder how I can be so sure. You must remember, I knew your father and he was a most honorable man. As they say, the apple never falls far from the tree."

"My father was here in this time?" Would the questions ever stop? Every time he got the answer to one, it simply created more.

"He was, and before you ask me why, I'll tell you what I know. He was in some danger back in your time. I don't know the specific details, but his life was on the line, much as yours was. He had the watch in his possession because it had been handed down to him by his father. He understood the workings of it and that it had been created hundreds of years prior to his receiving it. It was created by a great and powerful sorcerer and given to your ancestor with the intent that it only be used as a way to save the bearer from danger that could possibly wipe out the family line. So in order to save himself and the generations to come, he used it. The original owner had it crafted to his specifications and as you can see, it's quite beautiful. His intent was to keep the family line from dying out. It would be passed down from father to son and if for any reason the man found himself in peril he could traverse time to escape that danger. That is what your father did, but he realized that he had to bring it back to you, because if he didn't, you wouldn't have it in your moment of need. You are the last of that line Braeden." He waited a moment for Braeden to digest what he'd just been told. "Now there is one bad thing about you being here with the watch and that is that if Niall Campbell gets his hands on the watch, we'll not be able to stop him from using it and from wreaking havoc in our world."

"And how do you know I won't use the watch?"

"I don't. But as I've said, I know you to be honorable by virtue of the fact that you are your father's son and he was a good man, Braeden. I trust that if you do use the watch, it will only be because you absolutely must."

"There is much I dinnae ken about this world." Braeden placed the watch back in his sporran and gazed at John, hoping to find something in his face that would put him at ease.

"Don't worry, lad. You'll catch on. I can see that you're smart and canny. Observe everything and watch what you say. You will live here at the castle. You will have your own room, right next to Tessa's. We have a secret wing here that we call home. None of the guests to the hotel know where it is, let alone how to access it. There are only a chosen few who are allowed to enter. You will be one of them." John unlocked a drawer in his desk and removed an ornate key and a rigid piece of paper, rectangular in shape. "You will need both of these to enter, so be sure to bring them with you when you leave our residence." He handed them to Braeden who examined them and then placed them in his sporran.

"Will Tessa nae mind that I'll be following her?"

"She'll have no choice, but I'm not going to tell her of my misgivings about Danny. She'll believe that it is the gentlemen of The Society that I am concerned about." John poked at something on his desk.

"Yes, sir," a female voice said. "Kelly, send Tessa back in please."

"We'll speak again on a regular basis, Braeden. I'm counting on you. If you need anything, please don't hesitate to ask. And if you have any concerns about Danny or the Society, come to me immediately."

The doors swung open and Tessa walked in. Once again, Braeden found himself mesmerized by her very presence.

"Well, did you hire him?" She stood, hand on hip, head cocked, gazing at Braeden. "I did. He's to be your new bodyguard."

"What? I don't need a bodyguard, Dad." Tessa's casual stance turned to immediate anger as she was now glaring at her father.

"You may not think so, but I do. I have enemies here in Las Vegas and they know that the only thing I care about more than The Albannach, is you. I wouldn't put it past them to try to harm you or kidnap you in an effort to get to me."

Tessa wrinkled her brow and made a most unhappy face. Braeden was fascinated by her facial expressions. Her full lips were pouting now and he noted that she was clenching her fists at her sides. She was not happy about this and it was plain for all to see.

"Dad, I'm perfectly capable of taking care of myself. I certainly don't need this, this…" she stammered and stuttered, at a loss for words, but then found them. "This costumed Highlander following me around where ever I go."

"Braeden is a good man and one who is equipped to keep you safe. I expect to see him at your side when you leave the building, no matter where you are going and I won't hear another word about it."

Tessa harrumphed and looked away from John. Braeden sat waiting to see what would happen next. He was expecting a tantrum from the blonde beauty, but was surprised by what happened next.

"Okay, I guess." Tessa's final act of rebellion was to stomp her foot. "But I won't like it." She sent an icy glare Braeden's way and he looked away so she wouldn't see his amused reaction.

"Good. I knew you'd see it my way. And by the way, Braeden will be staying with us, so there's no chance you will be able to sneak away without him." John nodded at Braeden, who stood waiting for further instructions. "And Tessa."

"Yes, Dad," she said through gritted teeth.

"I love you." John held out his arms, calling her in for a hug.

"I love you too, Dad." Tessa softened her face and posture as she let her father envelop her in his arms.

"Show Braeden to his room, it will be the one right next door to yours. I've given him the keys and once he's gotten settled, you can show him around. And get him a McTavish kilt, please."

Tessa rolled her eyes at her father. Braeden was surprised at her small act of rebellion, but he'd seen his younger female cousins behave in a similar manner when their mothers and fathers had been stern with them about something they disagreed on. She next turned her disdain on him. "Come on then. I guess I'm stuck with you for the foreseeable future." She marched towards the doors and Braeden turned to look at John.

"Go on then. She's not going to make this easy for either one of us, but don't let her out of your sight. She may have agreed with me about this, but I know my daughter and she'll take the first opportunity she can to lose you."

"Aye." He was at her side before she had a chance to get to the doors that led down the long passageway.

"See you later, Kelly," Tessa called to her Dad's assistant.

"Bye." Kelly smiled sweetly at Braeden as he passed. "I'll be seeing you around." Braeden waved a hand in her direction, thinking he was going to have his hands full with Tessa McTavish.

"Pay attention to where we're going," Tessa instructed. "It's easy to get lost if you don't know your way around.

"I'll nae get lost, lass. I'll always have ye to show me the way."

CHAPTER 4

TESSA WAS QUITE peeved that her father had saddled her with this Scottish bodyguard. She wondered if it was really all about the Las Vegas Society of Magick and Sorcery, or if it had something to do with her engagement to Danny. She was very aware of the fact that he didn't like Danny, but this would be taking things to a whole new level for her father. If Braeden was going to be tagging along with her wherever she went, she'd never get to be alone with Danny and he wasn't going to like that. Even more importantly, she needed to be alone with Danny so she could try to understand why she'd suddenly decided she wanted to marry him. It was a conversation they needed to have, but one that required one-on-one time. So far every time she'd seen him with the intention of discussing it, she somehow ended up in what she referred to as a love haze. She didn't believe Danny would feel threatened by Braeden, especially since he had a huge female fan base, was a really good looking guy and a celebrity. However, Braeden was by far the more handsome of the two. He had smoldering good looks and that bad boy appeal that she loved. Apparently so did all the other women at The Albannach who'd been practically falling all over themselves to get a better look at him, and Kelly had barely been able to hide her appreciation as she bid them good-bye.

That gave Tessa an idea. If she could fix Braeden up with Kelly, perhaps she could manage to sneak away while he was occupied with her. She wasn't seeing Danny tonight, but she did have a date with him the next night, after his show. It was Valentine's Day and they'd planned a romantic night out on the town. It wouldn't be quite as romantic, but she couldn't help that. She'd call Kelly and invite her to join them. It was a perfect plan. She assumed Kelly was currently unattached as she hadn't heard her mentioning anything about a new boyfriend and since Kelly was always ready for a good time, this would be fun.

She guided Braeden through the maze of corridors that led them to a door where she waved a key card in front of the lock and it opened on its own. Braeden stared at it as if it had opened by some strange magic. Tessa loved the way the new keys worked. They'd used the same technology for the guest rooms as well.

They walked through into a secret garden filled with trees and flowers, which looked completely out of place in the Las Vegas desert. At the far end stood a beautiful arched wooden door surrounded by panes of glass that mimicked the Celtic Tree of Life and led to a two-story cottage reminiscent of the kind you'd find in the Scottish country-side, thatched roof and all. The Tree of Life was carved into the door and the branches extended to be etched into the glass. It was a master-piece. Just like the gate to the cashier's booth had been her creation, so had this magnificent door. The tree design was a perfect symbol for the hotel and had been used freely throughout the property. Braeden appeared suitably impressed as he took in his surroundings.

"The card opens the doors into the garden and the key is for this door." She took out her key and unlocked the door. It opened into an interior that was grand and yet cozy. She held the door for Braeden to enter and then closed it after him. "I'll show you to your room."

Tessa climbed an elaborately carved staircase up to the second floor, which consisted of her apartments. Her father's room was on the first floor, so they each had their own privacy. Or at least she'd *had* her privacy. She was now being forced to share it with Braeden MacDon-ald. She'd make the best of it though. Tessa wasn't one to dwell on the negatives of any situation, choosing to see things in a positive light whenever possible. She couldn't believe her father had hired this stranger to be her bodyguard. She was baffled as to what he was think-ing. "This is your room." She opened the door and he followed her in. "Make yourself at home. The kitchen is downstairs, although we rarely cook. The restaurants in the casino are really good and all you have to do is pick up the phone to order anything you'd like."

Braeden appeared confused by that, but he nodded his head in acknowledgement. "Are you hungry now? I don't know when you ate last, but it is past lunch time."

"Aye. I am hungry. I havenae eaten since yesterday." He had an al-most wistful expression on his face.

"Okay. It doesn't look like you have any belongings to leave here, so let's go get you some food. What would you like to eat? We've got sev-eral world class restaurants on the property." She waited for his answer, but he didn't seem to have one. "We've got Italian, Asian, American, French, Mexican and Scottish, of course. What will it be?"

"I dinnae ken."

"I'll decide then." Tessa glanced at him waiting for a response, but instead found him gazing into her eyes with an unreadable expression. She paused, drawn into a staring contest with him and after a moment where she felt herself inexplicably drawn to him, broke away. "Okay, then American it will be. I think you'll like it." As they left the room, Tessa pointed to another door a little further down the hall. "That's my room over there." As they approached, she opened the door revealing a neatly decorated space, with a private sitting room, a small fireplace and a window that looked out over the garden.

Braeden peeked his head in and seemed to focus on the bra and panties she'd dropped on the floor in her hurry to leave that morning. She blushed as she quickly scooped them from the floor, tossing them into the clothes hamper in her bathroom. Tessa turned back to find his focus had shifted to her, his eyes ablaze with something akin to desire. She dropped her gaze and placed an errant hair that had fallen into her eyes behind her ears. "Sorry about that. I guess I forgot to pick them up this morning." Peeking up at him again, their eyes met for a brief moment before his moved from her to the bed. Embarrassed by the thoughts floating through her head, she squeezed past him, leaving the room, and finding she was quite warm. She could feel him as he walked behind her and she wondered what thoughts might be going through *his* head. He exuded a raw sensuality. She could feel his gaze on her back as they walked and she found she enjoyed being the object of his attention. She peeked back at him over her shoulder, taken again with his masculine beauty and the fiery way he gazed into her eyes.

"Are you okay back there?" she managed to croak out between parched lips. Braeden nodded and Tessa wondered if he ever said more than two or three words at a time. "You don't talk much, do you?"

"Only when I've something to say, lass."

She had to admit, his deep Scottish burr and the way he called her 'lass' left her wishing he'd speak more often so she could wrap herself in the warmth of his voice as it vibrated through her body. As he walked ahead of her to get the door, she noted his muscular arms and the width of his back. She could almost picture him shirtless and it made her body hum with appreciation. She mentally scolded herself for going there. Braeden was an employee and she was technically his boss. More importantly, she was also engaged to Danny. She was practically a married woman for goodness sake. She hurried past him, and breathed in his scent, which was intoxicating. It wasn't any cologne she recognized, but it tickled her nose with its woodsy scent.

He walked close by her side the entire way to Johnny's Bar and Grill, occasionally he would lightly place a hand on the small of her back to guide her through the crowds, which shamefully sent shivers of delight through her body. The line at the entrance was long, but Tessa walked straight past and inside, drawing Braeden in her wake. People grumbled as they passed and she smiled as she noticed Braeden giving them a warning look. He certainly was taking his job seriously. The scowl he wore made him appear quite fierce and it was having a strange effect on her.

The hostess led them to a table in the back of the restaurant, which was reserved especially for Tessa and her father. The hostess handed them menus and walked away, but not before smiling sweetly at Braeden.

"Have whatever you like, Braeden. It's on Dad." She glanced up at him and the seductive glint in his eyes caused her to quickly open her menu and start reading.

Braeden examined his and then put it down. He scooped up the glass of water that had been placed in front of him and quickly downed the whole thing.

"What are you getting?" Tessa had closed her menu as well, signaling the waiter to come take their order.

"I dinnae recognize any of this food."

"I'm sorry. Maybe we should have gone to the Scottish restaurant." From the look of him she imagined he was probably like most red-blooded men. She opened her menu again searching for something she thought he'd enjoy. "You'd probably like the New York steak. Why don't you get that?"

The waiter arrived, pen in hand, ready to jot down their order. "My name is Joseph, I'll be your server. Are you ready to order, Miss McTavish?"

"Yes, Joseph. I'll have the chopped veggie salad." Tessa gave him the rest of the order. "Could we get more water for Mr. MacDonald?"

"Of course, I'll be right back with that."

Joseph walked away and Tessa sat back in the booth and watched what was happening in the rest of the room. After perusing the diners, she turned back to Braeden with a bright smile adorning her pretty face.

"You have a beautiful smile," Braeden noted.

"Thank you. I had a good orthodontist. I hated wearing braces at the time, but it was worth it in the end though." Why was she babbling about her teeth when a simple 'thank you' would have been enough.

"What is an orthodontist?" He carefully pronounced the word.

"You know. A doctor who helps straighten your teeth." She smiled again, showing him what she meant.

"That sounds painful. Was it?" He furrowed his brow as he spoke.

"Not really. It hurt my pride more than anything." Tessa followed Braeden's eyes as they flicked from one end of the room to the other. "Is everything alright?"

"Aye." He seemed to think further about her question. "Tessa, I feel out of place here. I dinnae ken why I'm here or even if I should be here."

She wasn't quite sure what to say to that. If he didn't know why he was there, then she sure didn't. "I guess you needed a job and my father saw something in you that made him hire you. My father's a brilliant businessman and he knows what he's doing, so even if you and I don't know why you're here, you can rest assured, he does." She hoped that helped and, wanting to reassure him, she reached out her hand to place it on his, realizing her mistake as he started at her touch and she quickly pulled away. Underneath his tough-guy exterior, there was something about Braeden that appeared so lost, and a bit sad. It made Tessa want to pull him in for a hug and to comfort him. It wasn't obvious when she first saw him because he seemed to be an expert at appearing unapproachable and dangerous, but as she spent time with him, she could feel it. She could see it in his eyes. Something had happened to him and it wasn't good. Maybe after he got to know her better he'd confide in her, but for now he was pulling at her heartstrings.

THE HEAT THAT shot up Braeden's arm at Tessa's touch caused him to jump. She'd caught him off guard. If he'd known, he wouldn't have moved a muscle, but he had and to his regret she'd quickly removed her hand. He'd hardly had time to savor the feel of her. He wanted her to touch him again, but he didn't know why she had touched him to begin with. He gazed into her vibrant blue eyes and held her there for a moment before she quickly looked away. It gave him time to examine her more closely. She was most pleasing to the eye. Her flaxen locks, her sapphire eyes and her sweet, full lips sent his mind wandering to places it shouldn't. He liked the way she seemed so sure of herself. She was confident that she didn't need his protection and he had seen the anger flare in her eyes when her father told her Braeden would be shadowing her wherever she went. Despite the fact that her father's wishes weren't her own, she would do as he wished. Braeden was sure she'd test him. He didn't know how or when, but it was obvious she didn't wish to have him with her at all times.

"Braeden, I have a date tomorrow night with my fiancé, Danny. It will be quite late. After his show. You don't have to come with me. Danny will make sure I'm safe."

Their food arrived and as the girl placed it on the table in front of them, he watched as Tessa looked everywhere but at him and then examined her food as if it were the most fascinating thing she'd seen all day. She thanked the lass and took a bite of the greenery in her bowl.

Curiosity had Braeden watching her every move. "Tessa, yer Da wishes me to be with ye. 'Tis no trouble to guard ye. I'll be sure to stay out of yer way." Date? Show? Everything she'd said was lost on him. However, the smell of the food that had been set in front of him had his mouth watering. He wasn't sure of the proper way to eat it, having never seen anything like it back home. He recognized the steak, but the other items on his plate were new to him.

"Would you like some ketchup?" Tessa asked.

"Catch up?" he asked, unfamiliar with the word.

Tessa handed him a bottle filled with red liquid. "For your fries." When Braeden didn't take it, she put it down next to his plate. "Okay, since you're stuck following me around, I have a better idea. What if I get Kelly to join us? It's Valentine's Day, but I don't think she has plans. You should bring flowers or something. Then you won't seem like you're watching me and Danny won't be bothered by you being there." She took another bite of her salad, watching him and waiting for his answer. She leaned forward, hands clasped beneath her chin, elbows resting on the table. "Well, what do you think?"

WHY WASN'T HE answering her? Maybe he didn't understand. They did seem to have somewhat of a language barrier happening between them. She tried again. "Kelly's joining us won't keep you from doing your job. It will just make it look less suspicious to whoever it is that my father is worried about, if they even exist." Braeden had one eyebrow cocked and was glancing at her with curiosity and perhaps a bit of suspicion. "You know what, let's just eat our lunch and we can discuss this later."

Tessa watched with some amusement as Braeden stared at his plate. He glanced at a nearby table where a man was enjoying a burger. After a moment of watching other diners, he picked up his knife and fork, finally taking a bite. The expression of wonder on his face had Tessa believing that he'd never had a steak before in his life. Either that or this one was the most delicious things he'd ever eaten.

"Is it good?" she asked, although her answer was written all over his face.

"Aye." He took another bite and closed his eyes, obviously savoring his meal. Tessa smiled and stifled a giggle as she watched him. He certainly wasn't hard to look at. He was really quite handsome and incredibly well built. His eyes, dark and penetrating, had been serious only moments before, but now they'd softened as he visibly relaxed. He tossed his shoulder length brown curls out of his face and shifted in his seat, his knees brushing Tessa's leg and settling alongside, barely touching her. She had the urge to move her leg to touch his. Tessa had a heightened awareness of his close proximity and found herself yearning to nestle into his arms, to feel his strength as he held her close. She fidgeted in her seat, her body buzzing from the static charge she felt rising from her leg, pulling it closer and closer. Sanity returned and Tessa coughed and moved her leg away, causing Braeden to focus those chocolaty-brown eyes on her reddened face.

"Is everything alright, lass?" He asked, concern in his voice.

Tessa cleared her throat. "Yes. Just a tickle in my throat. Nothing to worry about." This was going to be tough even though it shouldn't be. She had to see Danny. Maybe that was all she needed. Tomorrow night couldn't come soon enough.

CHAPTER 5

RELIEF SWEPT THROUGH Tessa as they left the restaurant behind. Being in such close proximity to her new bodyguard was wreaking havoc on her normally good sense and awakening a need in her that hadn't been met in a very long time. She and Danny hadn't consummated their relationship. He wanted to wait until they were married. Tessa didn't mind, although she thought it unusual in this day and age, but she also knew that for some people it was very important and apparently Danny was one of them. So she would be happy to do as he wished. Besides, she never really had those kinds of thoughts around him. It had been easy to this point, so why was she having them around Braeden. Something about his large, masculine frame and animal magnetism was causing Tessa a great deal of angst. If she let her mind wander, it went down a path that made her feel as if sex, in particular sex with Braeden, was always on her mind and was what she had to have if she was ever going to be able to function normally again.

For his part, Braeden always seemed to be eyeing her with an unreadable expression. Tessa could feel the palpable sexual tension between them, making her blood warm, and she knew he was feeling it too.

"This has got to stop." Tessa whispered to herself, but not as softly as she thought.

"What has to stop?" Braeden was at her elbow, eyes searching for some perceived danger.

"You weren't supposed to hear that. I was just talking to myself." Tessa groaned as his lips curled into the sexiest smile she'd ever laid eyes on. And damned if he didn't have dimples to boot. She wasn't sure how she was going to make it through the rest of this day if he didn't… if she couldn't… That kind of thinking was only going to serve to frustrate her even more than she already was. She closed her eyes and got a hold of herself, and head high, marched through the casino, determined to do what she'd set out to do and show Braeden around.

BRAEDEN DID HIS best to hide his amazement at everything he was seeing, including Tessa's sweet, sweet bottom as she walked in front of him. It was a lovely view and one he'd like to see more of. She'd seemed quite tense after they'd eaten lunch and he thought he knew why, but unfortunately she'd gotten herself under control and was now being the perfect guide. It would certainly be much more fun to spend the rest of the day in bed with Tessa McTavish than following her around The Albannach while she pointed out items she thought he should know about. Based on her feisty nature, he expected it would be quite an afternoon, but he would bide his time and enjoy making her uncomfortable while he waited.

From what he could tell, they were in the largest castle he'd ever seen and it was being used as an inn of some sort, although it was also unlike any inn he'd ever been to. Tessa called it a casino and resort. He understood that most of the people he came across, and there were more than he'd ever seen in any one place, were gambling. Some were at card tables and others at strange looking things Tessa called slot machines. They made ringing noises and lights flashed, mesmerizing those sitting in front of them. The lights were fascinating. He had no idea how they worked. They were definitely not candles.

As a matter of fact, the candles that were visible weren't what was lighting the windowless space they found themselves in. More magic he assumed. The people who worked at the casino were dressed in Scottish garb, although it was certainly different from what he was wearing. The women in particular were very scantily clad. Things had certainly changed in the three hundred years since his time.

"So you've never been to a casino before." Tessa was walking close by his side. So close in fact that at times she bumped into him in an effort to avoid the large crowds of people in the casino.

"Nay. I havenae." He grasped her elbow and guided her out of the path of a man who was obviously well into his cups and was staggering straight towards Tessa. She scooted closer to him and he put a protective arm around her shoulders, leaving it there as they continued. He was surprised when, instead of moving away, she melted into his side and stayed for a brief time. Braeden held his breath, afraid to do anything that might cause her to come to her senses and remove her warm, soft body from his side. But all good things must come to an end and Tessa, perhaps feeling a bit embarrassed, separated herself from him and began guiding him to an outdoor area. They passed through a wall of glass doors into the uncomfortable heat he remembered from his arrival. Shielding his eyes from the bright sunlight he followed Tessa down a path lined with plants and trees he was unfamiliar with. By now, he assumed everything he came across would be something he'd never seen before.

"This is the pool. Guests who are staying at the hotel use their key to gain entrance, they get their towels here." She pointed to the left at stacks of cloth being handed to people as they walked by.

Braeden was bored with everything about this tour with the exception of Tessa. Everyone seemed to have forgotten their clothing, but he understood now that in this strange place he'd been sent to that it was normal to dress this way. He wondered if Tessa ever dressed in so little clothing. Movement from beneath his kilt told him he'd best get his mind thinking about something other than Tessa or he was going to embarrass himself and her.

The oppressive heat, which had been thankfully missing while they were inside, had Braeden wishing he could discard his wool plaid and dive into the cool turquoise water of the pools, which looked very inviting. He remembered there was a smaller pool at the McTavish private residence. He'd like to swim there later. Mayhap Tessa would join him.

They continued walking through the pool area and then Tessa opened another gate with her key. "This is the wedding chapel. We've got weddings booked every day for the foreseeable future. We tried to create a traditional Scottish experience for the bride, groom and their guests. What do you think? Did we succeed?"

"Aye. Tis lovely."

"Come on. I'll show you where we teach archery and falconry and then we'll get you a McTavish plaid." Tessa walked on and Braeden followed, thinking all the while about dipping his hot, hard cock into some icy cold water to dampen the carnal urges he was having.

TESSA HAD COMPLETED the tour of the hotel and she led Braeden out through the front doors and onto Las Vegas Blvd. where they'd employed bagpipers to welcome people to The Albannach. She was about to ask Braeden what he thought of the hotel when she noticed him staring down the street towards King Arthur's Casino. His posture had stiffened and he appeared ready to charge off down the street, forgetting his duties as her bodyguard.

"Is everything okay?" Tessa took a peek at his face and was surprised to see it filled with rage. "Never mind, no need to answer. I can see that it's not."

"The castle of my enemies," he growled, low and ominous.

Tessa laughed uncomfortably. "Your enemies. I know they're our competition, but I wouldn't consider them our enemies."

"They may nae be your enemies, but they are surely mine, lass."

Tessa grabbed his arm and tried to turn him away and back towards The Albannach, but he easily resisted her attempts. As long as she had his arm in her hands, it couldn't hurt to enjoy the feel of the solid muscle beneath his shirt. She was impressed by his strength and realized she had no control over him whatsoever should he decide he was going to The King Arthur. It reminded her of the time her cousin's massive stallion took her for a walk around his pasture.

"Come on, Braeden, I think we should go see my father." She had to let her father know he'd hired someone with serious psychological issues. He had seemed somewhat normal up until this moment, but now Tessa wasn't sure her father was aware of everything he needed to know when he'd hired Braeden.

Braeden slowly turned his focus away from The King Arthur and faced her. "Aye. I must speak with yer Da."

Breathing a sigh of relief, Tessa made her way back through the doors and into the cool air of the casino lobby. Braeden was right behind her. She hurried towards the elevators and was happy that the one leading to her father's executive offices was waiting for them. They entered and once again, Braeden stood facing her. Apparently he didn't have any elevator etiquette. Tessa took his arm, spinning him so that he was facing the doors. He glanced back at her with a questioning look, but she didn't really feel like giving him a lesson in how to properly ride the elevator, so she said nothing. The doors opened and she practically ran to her father's office.

"Hello again," Kelly said as Tessa ignored her and went right into her father's office. Braeden was hot on her heels.

"Is something wrong, Tessa?" John McTavish asked.

"Something's weird is more like it. Dad, I gave Braeden a tour of the property as you asked and then we went out the front doors and he got all weird when he saw The King Arthur. He says they're his enemy and he looked like he was going to storm down there and kill someone."

John laughed and laughed, causing Tessa and Braeden to exchange concerned glances. When he finally stopped, he said, "Braeden, please sit. You too, Tessa."

"Braeden, I understand how you may have mistaken The King Arthur for an enemy castle, but believe me when I tell you, they are not your English enemy."

"Dad, what is going on here? The English and the Scots aren't enemies."

"Not any more." John directed his comments to Braeden. "We're in America, Braeden. The people at the castle down the street, which isn't a real castle by the way, are American and the Scots and the English are no longer enemies.

"Dad?" Tessa was getting anxious. What was her father talking about? Surely, if Braeden had ever picked up a history book or gone to school, he knew all of this. Not to mention he was from Scotland. He had to know it was part of Great Britain.

"Tessa, I'm going to tell you something that you may find hard to believe, but it's true. You know I'd never lie to you." John leveled his worried eyes on her.

"You're scaring me. What could be so unbelievable?" She gazed from John to Braeden and back again.

"Braeden has come to us from the past."

Again she glanced at her father and then at Braeden who sat stoically at her side. "What do you mean *the past*? Do you know him from when he was growing up?" Braeden wasn't much older than she was, so she assumed that was what her father must mean.

"He time-travelled here fresh from the Glencoe Massacre, brought here courtesy of a charmed pocket watch given to him by his grandmother."

Tessa could feel herself starting to hyperventilate. How could that possibly be true? Despite her initial reaction, she knew it had to be. Her father would never lie to her.

"Deep breaths, dear. Deep breaths. I know this goes against everything that we know to be true of our world, but there are some things going on here, right here in Las Vegas, that set the wheels in motion for Braeden to join us."

Braeden rose from his chair and squatted down in front of Tessa, taking her hand, a look of concern in his eyes. Tessa stared into his face. "He looks so real."

"I am real, lass. This has come as a shock to me as well."

She thought about the moment she'd first met Braeden and how confused he looked by everything. Suddenly all the awkward moments they'd shared this afternoon made perfect sense. "Amazing."

Braeden smiled up at her, causing her heart to beat even faster than it already was. "Are ye well, Tessa?"

"I'll be okay. I'm sorry. This must be so difficult for you and here you are worrying about me. I can't imagine finding myself in a different time and place, particularly one as strange as this."

"All will be well. I'm sure of it. It may take time, but this is my home now and I will learn to live here," he assured her.

Kelly's voice came through the intercom on John's desk. "Niall Campbell is here to see you."

Braeden jumped up practically knocking his chair over in the process. "Campbell?"

"Aye, lad. Niall Campbell. Let me find out why he's here. We spoke of it earlier and I know you've just been through an ordeal with the Campbell's, but try to remember that was a long time ago and had nothing to do with this man, although I don't trust him and I'm sure he's up to something. If the two of you would go into my conference room, I'll see what he wants. I'd prefer that he didn't know you were here, Braeden."

Tessa stood and walked to the hidden entrance behind her father's desk. She slid the panel to the side and motioned for Braeden to follow. He glanced quickly at the office door and scowled before following her. Tessa slid the panel closed behind him, effectively hiding the room and entrance from sight as they both stood, ears to the door.

"Niall, how good to see you. To what do I owe the honor of your visit?" John's voice came through the door loud and clear.

"John. 'Tis good to see ye as well."

"Sit, please. Can I get you something to drink?" The sound of ice cubes clinking in the glass filtered through the door.

"Aye. Thank ye. Congratulations on yer grand opening. It seems everything is going well. 'Tis quite a crowd ye have in the casino." Something about Niall's tone seemed insincere to Tessa.

"I'm very pleased. The hotel is completely booked for the next several months." Tessa could just imagine her father puffing out his chest with pride as he gave this information to Niall.

"That's verra good news," Niall responded.

Tessa repositioned herself closer to Braeden so she could hear more clearly. She could feel his disdain for Niall Campbell, even though they'd never met. His rigid stance was a clear sign.

"What can I do for you, Niall?" John got to the point of the visit.

"Well, I just wanted to alert ye to something unusual that has happened in Las Vegas today. I'm not sure exactly what it is, but there was an unusual ripple in the atmosphere. Did ye feel it?"

"No. I can't say that I did. I wonder what it could have been."

"Are you sure ye cannae feel it? It seems even stronger here at yer hotel. I was hoping ye might be able to tell me, but it seems ye're as in the dark as I am."

Braeden's muscle's twitched and his body tensed as he listened. He reminded Tessa of a mountain lion, ready to pounce on its prey. She hoped he'd do as John had asked and maintain control, but could see there was only a hair's breadth separating the two.

"I am." John answered. The silence that followed must mean the two were mulling this over while sipping their drinks.

Niall cleared his throat. "I should also let ye know there are some rumors going around that there are those who would love to see ye fail at yer new endeavor and would do anything to make it happen."

"Really. Ye wouldn't happen to know who that is, would ye?"

"I'm afraid not. As I said, it's a rumor; who knows if there's any truth to it. I just thought ye should know."

"Thank ye, Niall. I appreciate the information. Jealousy is one of the deadly sins for a reason."

Tessa could just imagine her father taking great pleasure in that small but obvious jab at Niall.

"Indeed." There was a pause and then. "Ye know I value yer friendship, John. I'd hate to see anything happen to ye or yer lovely daughter. Be vigilant, please."

"Of course. Thank you for your concern, but I'm sure my security people will take good care of us."

"Well, then. I'll be on my way." Tessa heard him put his glass down and walk to the door. "Good to see ye."

"You, too, Niall. Don't be a stranger."

Tessa and Braeden waited for a moment after hearing Niall leave the room, closing the door behind him.

"Tessa, you can come back in," John called.

"That was weird," Tessa observed as she and Braeden rejoined John.

"Yes." John appeared to be mulling things over as he wore a serious expression.

"What did he mean 'a ripple in the atmosphere'?" Tessa asked.

"I believe he felt the watch returning to Las Vegas."

"My pocket watch?"

"Yes. That watch." John tapped his fingers on his desk as he thought, something Tessa knew to mean he was anxious about what had just happened. "You know it has magical properties. We've talked about it."

"Aye. So he knows it's here." Braeden seemed concerned now as well.

"He knows it's here and he wants to get his hands on it. We can't allow that to happen." John exchanged looks with Braeden.

"But how does he know it's here?" Tessa was having a hard time wrapping her brain around this whole thing. First she finds out that

Braeden is from the past and now there's a magical watch that Niall Campbell wants and that Braeden apparently has.

"The watch is what brought Braeden to us, so it allows the person who possesses it to time travel. It also has the ability to stop time. At the very least, Niall and the Society have been exposed to its presence at some prior time so they are familiar with the sensation of the watch's power and can recognize it. There's a connection there and I wonder if that explains your father's sudden disappearance. I was surprised to learn he was gone, but assumed he'd gone back to his own time. Still it was curious to me that he left abruptly without saying goodbye."

"I still don't understand. How is it that *you* can feel it?" Tessa was trying her best to figure this out.

"Braeden's father spoke with me about the watch and so I've seen it and held it before today. I think once you have been exposed to the powers of the watch, you can feel it whenever it's near. I know this is a lot to digest, but give it some time."

"And what about his warning that someone might try to hurt you or me? Do you believe him?"

"I do. In fact, that is why I have Braeden watching over you."

"Dad, I told you I can take care of myself. I think it's more important for Braeden to protect you." Worry for John had her anxiously wringing her hands. She loved her father so much. What would she do if anything ever happened to him?

"Tessa, please don't argue with me over this. If it's true, then the best way to get to me is through you. Anyone who knows me will understand that." John shuffled through the papers covering his desk before organizing them into neat piles.

"Do you think that Niall was making a veiled threat?" she asked.

John met her gaze. "He may very well have been, but I have no way of knowing for sure. Time will tell. In the meantime, we all need to be vigilant." He stood and walked to Tessa, placing his hands on her shoulders and leaning in to kiss her forehead. "I love you more than you can understand, Tessa. If anything ever happened to you, my life would be over. Braeden will remain your bodyguard and we'll not discuss it again. Understood?"

"Understood." Tessa glanced at Braeden who was now standing by the windows overlooking the strip. She wasn't sure he had been listening to her conversation with her father. He seemed to be in his own little world. She could only imagine what he must think of everything he was seeing and experiencing. She'd try to be more understanding from now on. Having him guarding her still rankled, but she'd go along with her father's wishes, at least for now.

"Why don't you and Braeden go and rest. I need you to be wide awake tonight. The casino will be bustling even more than it is right now."

Tessa kissed her father's cheek and smiled warmly at him. "I love you, Dad."

John returned her smile and pulled her in for a hug. "Off with you now."

"Braeden, let's go." Tessa took Braeden by the hand without even thinking and led him from the office and down the corridor to the elevators. She felt his hand close around hers as they walked. She liked the way it felt. They fit together perfectly and once again she was forced to think about Danny and just what was going on with him. Realization struck. She had to tell him that she couldn't marry him.

Chapter 6

VALENTINE'S DAY WAS meant to be a big deal at The Albannach. There was a grand wedding planned for later in the day and Tessa saw to it that everything would be perfect for the bride and groom. She wouldn't be there for the reception, but her assistant, Melissa, was very capable and Tessa wasn't at all concerned about leaving her in charge. If there were any problems, Melissa knew she was only a phone call away.

There were plenty of other festivities happening throughout the resort as well. Everyone entering the hotel was handed a sprig of heather wrapped in McTavish plaid ribbon along with a small box containing a chocolate treat created by the hotel candy makers. Those guests staying at the hotel found a bouquet of flowers, along with a bottle of champagne in their rooms. The bar was serving a special Valentine's Day cocktail that was the prettiest pinkish-red with a chocolate heart sitting on the rim of the martini glass, created especially for the occasion by The Albannach mixologists. The restaurants, not wishing to be left out of the festivities, all had specials to suit the occasion. The Albannach was all about love today and every member of the staff was fully committed to making it an occasion to remember for their guests.

Tessa hadn't seen Braeden yet today, but she'd sure heard his name being mentioned by the casino staff. And from the sounds of it he was making quite an impression in the best possible way.

She found she missed his hulking presence following her everywhere she went, especially after spending the whole day with him yesterday. She'd certainly complained enough to her Dad and at times she'd been less than pleasant to him, but he took it in stride. She was his commanding officer and he was her warrior. She smiled thinking it was pretty funny that she could boss around a man twice her size, who looked pretty fierce most of the time, but who, she'd discovered, had a kind heart. He never questioned her except when he thought she might be trying to get away from him. Tessa promised she wouldn't leave the building without him and so far she'd kept that promise, leaving him to do some security work where it was actually needed.

As Tessa reached the bottom of the escalator, her heart skipped a beat as she saw him standing by the Black Jack tables. He was easy to spot, standing easily a foot taller than most of those in the vicinity. She decided her self-imposed avoidance of him was over and she made her way directly to him. As she got closer, one of the cocktail waitresses approached and he smiled down at her, listening to what she had to say.

"I'm afraid I cannae join ye as I must go with Tessa tonight." Braeden politely answered and to Tessa's ear sounded disappointed.

The waitress looked crestfallen, pouting at him and leaning closer so that her body leaned into his arm.

"Don't you both have work to do?" Tessa asked.

"I'm sorry Miss McTavish." The young woman scurried away, but not before winking at Braeden as she went on her way.

"You shouldn't encourage that behavior. This isn't a dating service, you know. If you want to socialize you can do it on your own time." She could feel her blood boiling and knew she was over reacting, but somehow couldn't contain it.

Braeden's smile vanished and his expression became unreadable. "I apologize, but my time is nae my own, lass."

"You could always not follow me when I leave the hotel. That would free up some time for you." Tessa snapped back, but then returned to a more controlled approach. "I mean, if you really want to go with her tonight, I'm sure I'll be fine."

"'Tis my job to follow ye, Tessa."

He had her there. Braeden's calm, rational approach made her even more irritated with him, or was it herself she was irritated by. At any rate, she'd be better off dropping it, because if she examined her motivation, she could see it all pointed to one thing —jealousy.

THE LASS WAS jealous. That pleased him, but he'd not show her it had. She began to walk away and he moved to follow.

"We're not leaving the hotel, so you can do whatever it was you were doing before I arrived." She was upset with him. He'd need to be blind not to notice. Tessa avoided eye contact as she continued marching to get away from him.

"That would be speaking with Katie. Isnae that permitted?" He was enjoying himself, perhaps a bit too much.

"That's not what I meant and you know it." Turning to face him she narrowed her eyes suspiciously and crinkled her nose, which he found irresistible. He couldn't help but chuckle.

"I was keeping a watch on the gaming tables, lass, but it's time to move on." His serious demeanor was back.

"Do you know how to play Black Jack?" Tessa glanced up at him and he could see her irritation with him had passed.

"I do now. We have a similar game in my time. 'Tis called thirty-one." Much like Black Jack, where the goal was to get as close as possible to twenty-one, thirty-one had players collecting cards to end with a hand as close to thirty-one as they could get. He found that thinking about it had him missing his friends and family. Would it ever get any easier? He doubted it would.

"Do you know why the call it Black Jack?" she asked.

"Nae. Should I?" She appeared ready to tell him in any case.

"Most people probably don't know, but back when the game first came to America from France, it was called twenty-one or vingt et un. In order to pique the interest of gamblers, they made it so that if you got a black jack and an ace of spades, you'd win more money. The odds were ten to one and that's where the name Black Jack came from. I love trivial little facts like that. Don't you think it's interesting?"

"Aye. Verra." As far as interesting went, there had been many more things he'd seen in the last two days that he found much more interesting than that bit of information, but he'd not disappoint her by saying so.

She didn't object to his presence, so he continued walking with her. As they moved through the casino he kept watch. As the day went on he found he'd become busier. He was amazed how many times he'd had to pick someone up from the floor and how many times he'd had to rescue the cocktail waitresses from over zealous male patrons who'd forgotten how to keep their hands to themselves. One look at Braeden and they left without quarrel. The lasses were grateful for his help and so a chorus of "Braeden!" accompanied by smiles and waves followed him as he walked alongside Tessa. He was enjoying her annoyance. Every time his name was called she sent an angry glare in the direction of the lass who'd called out. He could've explained the reasons for their attention, but he was having much too much fun watching Tessa McTavish squirm.

As they passed the Skye Bar, the bartenders also called to him and waved. He was starting to feel more at home despite the absurdity of his situation.

"Looks like you've made some new friends."

He didn't reply. There was nae need. Her observation was correct and Braeden didn't feel the need to speak simply for the sake of filling the silence when it wasn't necessary.

Tessa stopped abruptly and faced him. He gently tucked a piece of her golden tresses behind her ear as he gazed into eyes as blue and fathomless as the ocean. He let his hand linger, wanting more than anything to kiss her plump, pink lips and imagining how soft they'd be and how sweet they'd taste to his own.

"I have some things to attend to in my office," Tessa stammered. "I'll see you later."

"Aye. Ye shall." He watched as Tessa walked away, realizing he could stand there all day. She was a lovely sight to behold.

His thoughts were interrupted by the sounds of breaking glass and an angry male voice. He turned to see Katie retrieving her tray from the floor and attempting to pick up the broken glass. She'd already cut herself in the process and was cringing as the threatening man berated her.

"That's what you get for ignoring me. I said I wanted another drink." The man glared down at her.

Katie was near to tears now as Braeden helped her to her feet and placed himself between her and the belligerent man.

"Get out." Braeden's controlled anger was apparent, but the man was either too drunk or too stupid to realize the danger he was in. He really had no idea who he was dealing with.

Good sense, if he'd ever had any, must have left the drunken bastard. He stood as tall as he possible could and though he was a good foot shorter than Braeden, he poked a finger in his chest. "You can't tell me to leave. Hell, I'm an American and you barely speak English."

"Get out." Braeden growled. He wanted this man gone so he could get Katie some help. She was bleeding all over her white blouse. When the man didn't budge, Braeden grabbed him by the shirt collar and lifted him off the ground. Now face to face with this drunken idjit. "Perhaps ye didnae hear me the first time, or the second. Get yer sorry arse out of here before I put my foot to it and send you out the door that way." His voice was low and menacing. The man appeared to finally understand how close he was to being beaten to a pulp. He opened his mouth to speak, but no words escaped his quivering lips.

Two security guards arrived and Braeden dropped the man, who scrambled to his feet and was quickly taken into custody by the guards.

"Take him out and make sure he doesnae come back." Braeden glared threateningly at the man who visibly cowered in the face of Braeden's wrath. He turned his attention to Katie and softened his demeanor, noting that she'd already been frightened enough. He didnae wish to cause her any more dismay. "Yer in need of bandaging, lass. Come with me."

"But what about the glass. Someone might get cut on it." Her voice trembled and tears brimmed in her eyes.

Braeden signaled one of the other waitresses. "Can ye see to it that this is cleaned up?"

She nodded. "Are you okay, Katie?"

"I'll be alright. I just cut myself on the glass," she managed to stammer out. Braeden wrapped a protective arm around her shoulders and walked with her to the private 'employee only' area of the casino. The poor lass was shaking like a leaf and he did his best to put her at ease.

There was a nurse and doctor on duty, part of a medical team who were available at all times, so it wasn't long before Katie was bandaged up. Braeden stayed by her side, sensing she was still frightened by what happened.

"Katie, are you okay?" Melanie O'Connell, the floor supervisor for the cocktail waitresses ran into the nurse's office. "I came as soon as I heard. What happened?"

"Some jerk who was way over the limit wanted another drink and I told him I couldn't serve him. He got pretty irate and he knocked my tray out of my hands."

"She cut her herself picking up the broken glass," the nurse offered.

"Is he gone?" Melanie looked to Braeden.

"Aye. He won't be back today or any other. I'll see to it."

"Katie, I think you should go home for the day. You've had a very trying experience. Go get changed and I'll see to it that someone walks you to your car."

"I'll take care of her," Braeden assured Melanie. "Go on, lass. I'll wait here for ye and I'll see to it that ye get to yer car without anyone bothering ye."

TESSA WAS DISMAYED to once again see Braeden walking with Katie. Only this time he had an arm around her. They were headed to the parking garage from what she could tell. The jealousy she felt earlier was back and she couldn't tamp it down no matter how hard she tried.

"What is he doing?" she asked.

"I'm sorry, what was that. I couldn't hear you over the music." Zach was wiping down the bar. "Can I get you a drink, boss lady?"

"No. Thanks, Zach."

"Were you asking me a question before?"

"Not really. I was talking to myself."

"That's not a good thing, is it?"

"Probably not." She tried to make light of it and she hoped Zach was buying it. "I'm kind of tired and I've still got so much to do and I was wondering what Braeden was doing with his arm wrapped around Katie." That last part just slipped out. "I was just running it all over in my head, but I guess I was saying it out loud."

"Yeah. I get it. I do that sometimes. I think Braeden was escorting Katie to her car. I guess you didn't hear what happened." He polished a few glasses before putting them away.

"No. Tell me." *This should be interesting*, she thought.

"Katie cut herself after some jerk knocked her tray out of her hands. She was pretty shaken up. Braeden took care of the guy though."

"Oh, good." Tessa was relieved to hear this. "Just doing his job."

"Yes, ma'am. He's great at it too. We haven't had any problems in the bar all day today."

Tessa smiled now that she knew Braeden was simply taking care of Katie and there wasn't a romance blossoming between the two of them.

"You got plans tonight? It's Valentine's Day, you know?" Zack continued putting drink orders together for the cocktail waitresses.

"I do know and I do have plans. How about you?"

"Nah. Life's too short and there are lots of women out there I haven't met yet."

"You'll change that tune before too long." Tessa shook her head and chuckled at him. He was good looking enough that she was sure he'd never have to worry about being alone. "There's more to life than seeing how many notches you can put in your belt. There's something to be said for having that one person you can come home to. The person who's going to be there through thick and thin. I look forward to the day when I have that person I can share my life with, not just drinks and a roll in the sack."

Zach appeared surprised by her candor. "You don't seem like that kind of girl."

"I'm not, which is why I'm hoping to…" She caught herself just as she was about to say *find that someone soon*. Hadn't she already found him? She was engaged to Danny Madden. The man of her dreams, or at least he was when she was with him.

"Why the scowl?" Zack said as he examined her face.

"Oh. It's nothing. I just remembered something I have to do." She turned away to leave.

"Tessa." Zach called to her as she left. "Happy Valentine's Day!" Smiling the smile that was surely a heartbreaker to every woman he met, Zach handed her a velvety rose of the deepest red.

"Why thank you, Zach. That's very sweet, but are you sure there isn't someone else you'd rather give this too?"

"Nope. I've got a bunch of them back here, I like to keep the ladies happy."

"Be careful. If you make them too happy, you might find yourself in a relationship before you know it." She smelled the rose appreciatively. Her favorite flower. "Mmm…" She wondered once again about seeing Braeden with Katie and why she cared so much.

☌

AS TESSA DRESSED for her night out, a night that was meant to be a romantic evening alone with her fiancé, she found herself thinking about Braeden and not the man she was supposed to marry. No matter how hard she tried, when she thought of herself in the warm embrace of the man she loved, she saw herself with Braeden. When she saw herself kissing the man she loved, she saw herself with Braeden. When she pictured the face of the man she loved, she pictured Braeden. Danny was the man she was going to marry, so why was she having all these romantic thoughts about Braeden. He was handsome, he was strong, he was kind and she'd felt something with him that she'd never felt with Danny, and that spelled nothing but trouble.

"What is wrong with you?" She found she was talking to herself again. She shook herself from head to toe, trying to erase the thoughts going through her head. She knew she was going to have to break it off with Danny, but would she be able to do it tonight. She felt terrible about it. Was she too nice for her own good, because the thought of hiking through the desert on the hottest day of the year would be preferable to breaking Danny's heart, especially on Valentine's Day? She already knew she should have never said yes to his proposal, but somehow, without conscious thought, it had simply escaped her lips. From the moment Danny slipped that engagement ring on her finger she was doomed. She would have gone along with the marriage no matter what, no matter how much she didn't want to, that is until Braeden MacDonald showed up in her life. Now she knew beyond a shadow of a doubt what she must do. It would be difficult, but it had to be done. It wasn't fair to Danny to be with someone who didn't really love him. He'd understand, wouldn't he?

She finished dressing and headed to Braeden's room feeling as if she were heading to her own funeral. She knocked, anxious to see his face and hear his voice. How could she have fallen so hard for him in such a short time unless it was meant to be? That must be it. He was here for her and she would gladly be his, now all she had to do was tell Danny.

CHAPTER 7

ANNY'S SHOW WAS just getting out as Tessa, Braeden and Kelly pushed their way through the crowds to the back of the theater. The hallways were empty with the exception of hotel security, and knowing who Tessa was, they merely nodded their heads as she and the others passed by on their way to Danny's dressing room door.

Tessa knocked. "Danny?" This was it. It was now or never.

"Come on in," Danny called. He was seated at his dressing table wrapped in a robe and removing his stage make up.

"I hope you don't mind. I brought some friends along with me." They all entered, closing the door behind them. "You know Kelly and this is Braeden. He's here visiting from Scotland."

"Nice to meet you," Danny said in a somewhat disinterested voice. He didn't even look their way.

"How was your show tonight?" Tessa was a bit nervous about what she knew was coming and embarrassed by his behavior. She didn't say anything, assuming he was surprised she'd brought people with her. She planned on talking to him later about their engagement. It wasn't going to be pleasant, but she felt she needed to do it.

"It was great, as always. The audience ate it up." He finished wiping his face off and stood, noticing Braeden for the first time. "You're from Scotland, huh?"

"Aye."

"How are you liking Vegas so far?" He didn't wait for an answer. "I see you've already found a pretty girl, nice work."

Braeden glared at him. Tessa could feel the tension in the air as the two men appraised each other. Kelly could feel it as well, glancing from one man to the other.

"Braeden, maybe we should wait outside and give Tessa and Danny some time alone." She headed for the door and Braeden appeared reluctant to follow. "Come on." She smiled sweetly at him and he relented.

46

Once they were out of the room, Tessa said, "Danny you were being rude."

"Was I? I didn't think so, but if I was, no big deal." He continued his after show rituals and poured himself a drink, not bothering to offer Tessa one.

"Well, it's a big deal to me. This is the first time you're meeting Braeden, try to be nicer," she scolded.

"You're not my mother," was his curt response. "I wasn't expecting you to bring an entourage along with you tonight. It's Valentine's Day. I thought it would be just you and me." He rose and kissed Tessa's cheek.

"I'm sorry. My dad asked me to show Braeden around and I thought things would go better if he had a date, so I asked Kelly."

Danny removed his robe revealing a thin, but muscular build in his boxer briefs. Tessa noted that seeing him this way did nothing for her. Her heart certainly didn't beat any faster, like it did when she saw Braeden fully clothed. Danny grabbed a shirt from a nearby hanger and put it on. "You could have given me a heads up. You know I don't like being caught off guard." He moved back across the room to Tessa and held her face in his hands, staring into her eyes.

A strange feeling came over Tessa as she spoke. "I don't know how many times I have to say I'm sorry. Can we just let it go and enjoy the rest of the evening? I don't want you to be angry with me." Tessa had been irritated with Danny, but was now inexplicably drawn to him. The side of Danny she'd just seen was one she didn't enjoy, but suddenly it didn't matter. There was a battle going on in her brain. She'd just been thinking that Danny behaved like a spoiled little boy at times, somehow making her feel like it was all her fault. Maybe it was. Maybe she was the difficult one. She tried without success to remember all the reasons she couldn't possibly marry him. But realized she wanted to marry him. She loved him. She felt herself drowning in his eyes as he continued to hold her with his stare.

"I would have enjoyed it better without the company, but we'll let it go for now." At first she thought all this eye contact was weird, but then she felt herself relaxing and couldn't imagine why she'd been so upset with him before. He was probably right. It was her fault. Here he was, her husband to be and she was treating him poorly. Danny moved away from her and pulled on a pair of jeans and then stepped into his shoes. "I had planned a nice romantic dinner for two, but that's obviously not going to work."

There was a knock on the door and Danny opened it. It was Tanya, his assistant. "Thanks for the roses, sweetie. She was just about to kiss his lips when he abruptly turned his head so her lips met his cheek. Tessa knew Tanya hadn't seen here standing there.

"Hi, Tanya."

"Oh, hi Tessa. I didn't see you there." Based on the fake smile she'd plastered across her face, Tessa could see she wasn't happy. "I'll talk to you later," she said to Danny as she ran a finger along his jaw.

"Later," Danny said, closing the door behind her.

"That was weird. Why did you get her flowers?"

"They were supposed to be for you, but the florist dropped them off in her dressing room instead of mine. I couldn't bear to tell her they weren't for her. She was so excited to get them."

"She knows we're engaged, doesn't she?"

"Of course she does, but I can't help it if she wants me."

Tessa's brain was feeling muddled, so she decided to drop it. "I don't know where you were thinking of going tonight, but we can always go to Hoy at The Albannach. Tonight's opening night. It should be a lot of fun." She waited, hoping for a positive response.

Danny made a face to show his displeasure. "It wouldn't be my first choice, but if it's what you really want I guess we can go."

"Good. You'll have fun. Besides, the local papers will be there and it would be good publicity for your show." She knew that would work in her favor.

"I don't really need the publicity, but I guess you can never have too much." He took one final look in the mirror, adjusting his shirt and jacket. "Damn. You are one lucky lady, Tessa.

She felt like an angel was guiding her on one shoulder and a devil on the other. The devil made her think - I am, while the angel said, "Run."

KELLY WAS SMILING up at him again. She really was verra pretty with her red hair and green eyes, but as she'd informed Braeden as soon as they were alone together, she had a boyfriend. He was happy she'd brought it up, but despite the fact she was a beauty and quite a lot of fun, that wasn't what Braeden was here for. He was supposed to keep an eye on Tessa. That was his main focus. She was closed up in that room with Danny who, while he didn't know him well, didn't impress Braeden as being the kind of man that John McTavish would approve of his daughter marrying. As a matter of fact, *he* wouldn't approve of it either. He'd keep careful watch on the two of them and intervene if this Danny fellow did anything inappropriate.

"You look so serious," Kelly was saying.

"Aye." He was sure the scowl on his face was giving him away.

"Are you not happy about having to spend time with me?" The fact that they'd been thrown together hadn't escaped either one of them and Kelly appeared to want Braeden to know she didn't mind the forced pairing.

"Nay. I'm verra happy to spend time with ye, Kelly. I'm also doing my job. I'm to keep an eye on Tessa." He nodded his head towards the door of Danny's dressing room.

"I know. John doesn't trust Danny and he's not very happy about the engagement."

"He's a disagreeable sort from what I've seen so far."

"He must be different when it's just the two of them, because I can't imagine what she sees in him otherwise."

The door flew open abruptly, causing Kelly to jump right into Braeden's arms. He protectively closed them around her as Tessa and Danny came out.

"Well, don't you two look cozy?" Danny gave them a cursory glance as he breezed past them and Tessa appeared surprised and maybe even a bit jealous to Braeden's eye. He set Kelly away from him, but kept an arm around her as they followed Danny and Tessa out of the building.

DANNY WAS IN an unusually bad mood. He was typically a lot happier to see Tessa and she wondered what was wrong.

"Is everything alright, Danny?" She hurried to catch up to him as they headed to his limo.

"Yes. Why wouldn't it be?"

The chauffeur opened the door and Danny stood aside while Tessa got in.

"I don't know. You just seem a bit edgy to me. Did I do something to upset you?"

"You mean other than bringing your friends along to ruin my plans for a romantic evening alone with you?"

Tessa felt badly about the situation and was doing her best to make up for it.

"We'll have a few drinks together and then maybe you and I can slip away without them noticing." Tessa knew that wouldn't be easy. Every time she looked up, Braeden had his eyes trained on her. He really takes his job seriously. She'd have to be sure to thank her father for his unnecessary concern. Danny wouldn't let anything happen to her, would he?

Why did that doubt enter her mind? She glanced Danny's way and he was staring at her oddly again. The negative thoughts she'd had about him earlier vanished and she smiled lovingly at him. Suddenly she remembered he'd always been a perfect gentleman and up until tonight, he'd been the ever attentive and loving boyfriend. Looking away, the negativity returned. She hoped this wasn't a glimpse into what she had to look forward to as his wife, because if it was there was no way she was marrying him. These Jekyll and Hyde feelings she was having were concerning. Brooding, she sat back in her seat and watched as Braeden helped Kelly into the limo before entering himself. She could see him eyeing the interior. The concerned look on his face told her that he was wary of this new mode of transportation. He sat next to Kelly and placed an arm across the back of the seat. To Tessa's mind he sat a little too close and Kelly didn't appear as if she'd be moving, which for some reason had Tessa raising an eyebrow in her direction. Kelly ignored her and as the limo drove off, turning sharply out of the parking lot, Kelly fell into Braeden, placing a hand on his knee. Tessa hoped it was simply to steady herself, but her hand remained where it had landed. *What does she think she's doing? I only invited her so Danny wouldn't be mad about Braeden following me around. If she gets any closer to him she'll be sitting in his lap.*

Braeden leaned down and whispered something in Kelly's ear, which made her giggle and made Tessa fume. Why she was getting upset over Kelly and Braeden was beyond her. She was engaged to Danny. Just because he was out of sorts tonight was no reason for her to start looking at Braeden as anything more than her bodyguard, but it was too late. She already had, and now she'd made the mistake of fixing him up with Kelly.

The limo headed down Las Vegas Boulevard to the private entrance at the back of The Albannach, where it was parked and the driver got out to open the door for them.

"How'd it go yesterday?" Danny asked, seeming genuinely interested in something for the first time this evening.

"Really well. I can't wait to see the club filled with people." Up until now, Tessa had only seen it as an empty, but beautiful room. It was fashioned after a castle great room. As a matter of fact, it had started off in the plans as an exact replica, but was then modified to accommodate the Las Vegas club scene. The bar was made of the finest mahogany and had plenty of stools for patrons. Tables were set around the room in a semi-circular pattern, leaving room for a dance floor.

Private booths were separated from the tables on an upper level. They were reserved for those who wanted a more pampered experience. To-night they'd have live music from a local Celtic Rock Band with a dee-jay who'd fill in for them while they took breaks. The club was at the very top of the hotel with a 360-degree view of Las Vegas. It was spec-tacular and as they departed the elevator, the lines waiting to get in were long and filled with people excitedly chattering. As they saw Danny pass, squeals of delight emitted from several of the women in the line, followed by those calling his name. Danny smiled, shook hands and even signed an autograph or two, but as soon as they were inside, he let Tessa know how much it bothered him to have to deal with his fans away from the show.

"I hate that I can't go anywhere without people demanding my auto-graph. I wish they'd just leave me alone." He harrumphed his way across the floor to the upper level of private booths.

"Danny, if they did that I doubt you'd have a job. After all, they love you and love your show. It doesn't hurt to give a little back, don't you think? I know you like your privacy, but in your line of work it's not always possible to avoid your fans." Tessa was practically running to keep up with him. She wished she'd worn more practical shoes. Her strappy heels weren't made for this pace.

Braeden appeared suitably confused as he followed along behind them and occasionally grasped Tessa's elbow so she wouldn't fall. She was impressed with what a gentleman he was. He was not only taking care of her, but held onto Kelly so she didn't get lost in the crowd.

"Being a celebrity is very difficult," she explained to Braeden, tip-ping her head and asking with her eyes if he understood what she meant.

"He's like the king," he simply stated.

"Elvis?" Danny perked up. He'd apparently heard Braeden's statement and assumed he was talking about Elvis Presley. "Thanks for the compli-ment. I don't sing, but I like to think of myself as the king of magic."

They were all seated now and a young woman in a tiny tartan ap-proached with a bottle of their finest champagne. Tessa spoke with her for a moment before seating herself next to Danny. She smiled happily at him and noted the same intense stare he'd given her earlier. *He's go-ing to make a good husband.* She glanced away and out towards the dance floor. Where had that thought come from? *Seriously, Tessa, you need to figure this out. One minute you want to break off the engagement and the next you're madly in love.* She had an unsettled feeling in the pit of her stomach as she wondered what exactly was wrong with her.

೦ಿ

"WOULD YOU LIKE to dance with me?" Kelly asked Braeden as she looked up at him with hopeful eyes.

Braeden perused the dance floor and then shook his head. He had no idea what was happening on the dance floor, but he preferred not to be a part of it. Kelly's disappointment was obvious and he felt badly for turning her down, but this was not the dancing that he was familiar with and he didn't want to leave Tessa alone with Danny. He'd already noted her change in mood from moment to moment and suspected Danny had something to do with it.

"Maybe after you have a drink and relax you'll change your mind." Kelly was smiling at him again. He was relieved she wasn't angry. "Oh, look. There's Sean!" She stood and waved at someone across the club. "Sean! Over here!"

"Is that Sean from The Royal Tournament?" Tessa glanced at Kelly and then at Braeden.

"Yes. Didn't I tell you I was seeing him?" Kelly asked. "I thought I did."

"No. You didn't, or I wouldn't have invited you to be Braeden's date tonight." Tessa was looking and sounding quite grumpy.

"I'm sorry. Sean's okay with it. I told him what we were doing and suggested that maybe he join us. You don't mind, do you Braeden?"

"Of course not, lass." He was actually relieved her man had arrived. Kelly was a lovely young lass, but he wasnae interested in being anything more than friends with her and with her man approaching he could focus his attention on Tessa and Danny."

Sean strode up the stairs to their booth. "Hey. Danny, Tessa." He nodded at them before squeezing into the booth next to Kelly who looked quite happy to have him there. "You must be Braeden. I'm Sean." He held out his hand to Braeden, who accepted the handshake. "I hear you're from Scotland."

"Aye. 'Tis true." Braeden noted that Sean was quite tall and had a warrior's build. Kelly was dwarfed as she sat between them, but was smiling brightly. "I'm so happy you're here. I couldn't get Braeden to dance with me, but now that you're here…"

"Sure. I'll dance with you, babe. Let me get a drink and then we'll dance as much as you like."

"What would you like?" Tessa asked.

"Scotch rocks, please." Sean answered. "I can order it. No worries."

"You're going to love this. We've installed apps here at the tables so we can order without having to leave our seats." She asked everyone else what they wanted to drink. "Done. The drinks will be here before you know it."

"Isn't it amazing?" Kelly asked. "You never have to wait for someone to make their way to your table to get your order again."

Their drinks were delivered within minutes of Tessa placing the order. One of the tiny-kilt wearing lasses placed their drinks in front of them. "Can I get you anything else?"

"No. We're good for now," Tessa answered.

"I love it." Sean held up his glass. "A toast to new friends and old."

They all clinked glasses and drank. Braeden took a large sip of his whiskey and savored the smoky goodness as it warmed its way to his belly.

"Braeden, you should come watch us practice for the show. I think you'd enjoy it. You might even want to participate." Sean appeared hopeful that Braeden would say yes.

"He's right, Braeden, you'd feel right at home." Tessa smiled knowingly at him and then turned to Sean. "We'll come by some time this week."

Braeden had no idea why Tessa thought he'd feel right at home at this practice, but it was part of his job to follow her wherever she went and if she wished to do this, then he'd be forced to join her.

"Great. The guys will be stoked. They love it when we have guests, especially guests who wouldn't mind sparring with us." He put his arm around Kelly. "You ready for that dance?"

"Yes!" She practically pushed him out of the booth. Laughing, Sean pulled her close and they walked down the stairs to the dance floor.

Braeden watched with interest as the two moved to the unusual music.

"You should really give it a try." Tessa's voice interrupted his thoughts. "You'd have fun."

Braeden was sure he didn't wish to make a fool of himself before all these people. "Nae. I dinnae think so."

"Danny, let's dance." Tessa grabbed his hand and he quickly pulled it away. "Not now," was his curt reply.

Braeden had the impression that this Danny was not as interested in Tessa as he led her to believe. Her father would be interested to hear this. How could a man love a woman and not wish to give her everything she wanted and more? If Tessa were his woman, he would gladly dance with her no matter that he'd appear a fool doing so.

"Damn. No one will dance with me." Tessa seemed quite saddened by this.

"Come, lass. I'll dance with ye." Knowing he might regret this, Braeden stood and offered Tessa his hand. She took it, never once glancing back to see Danny's reaction.

They made their way onto the dance floor just as a nice, slow song began to play. Braeden took a moment to observe the other dancers before pulling Tessa into his arms. She wrapped hers around his neck and smiled up at him. He was going to enjoy this verra much.

"Thank you for dancing with me." Her soft, sultry voice shot straight to his core. "'Tis my pleasure, lass. Ye are a beautiful treasure and if ye wish to dance, then I am at yer service."

"I don't know what's wrong with Danny tonight. Or maybe it's me. I feel like one minute I love him and the next I don't like him very much at all. I wish I could explain it better."

"No need. I can see yer dilemma. Do you nae wish to marry him?"

"I don't and I was going to tell him tonight, but every time he looks at me it's as if I'm under some crazy spell and I can't think clearly."

"Mayhap ye are under a spell." Braeden didn't mention John's thoughts on the subject.

"I can't imagine that's even possible." Tessa gazed up at him, worry in her eyes. "Do you really think it's possible?"

"Aye. I do, and if ye think about it, nothing is too far fetched when ye consider I've travelled here from another century, aye?"

Tessa chuckled at his statement. "True. What can I do about it though? I mean if he really did put a spell on me. Every time I try to say something about it, he gives me this look and I forget what I was going to say."

Braeden thought about this for a moment. "He must be reinforcing his spell each time."

"I can always break up with him via text I suppose, although I think that's an awful way to end things." She seemed to think about this a bit more. "I get the feeling he doesn't even like me, so it probably wouldn't hurt his feelings too much."

"'Tis nae his feelings I'm concerned with. 'Tis ye. What is it that he wants from ye?"

"Good question. I wish I knew."

Braeden could have danced with Tessa like this forever. The feel of her soft, warm, womanly body pressed close to his sent lustful thoughts coursing through him. The fact that his hardened manhood was pressing into her belly didn't seem to bother her and while it was causing him a good deal of painful pleasure, Braeden wasn't in any hurry for it to end.

"Braeden?" Tessa's voice seemed filled with the same lust he was feeling. "Aye, lass."

"Never mind. It's nothing." She rested her head on his chest completely unaware of the change in music. Everyone around them danced to a lively tune while they were still wrapped in each other's arms. Gazing up to their private table, Braeden saw Danny glaring down at them as they danced.

"Yer man seems upset."

Tessa looked up. "Oh, no. That's not good." She pulled away from Braeden and headed for the stairs.

Braeden grabbed her hand, stopping her. "Dinnae do anything yet. I'm afeared of what he may do if ye tell him ye dinnae wish to be with him."

Tessa nodded her agreement and Braeden breathed a sigh of relief. He would have to keep close watch on this Danny Madden. They must discover if he was in league with Niall Campbell and if so why.

CHAPTER 8

KELLY'S BRIGHT SMILE greeted them as they approached John's office, eliciting a wink from Braeden.

"Good morning." Tessa said, glancing from Kelly to Braeden.

"Good morning. Your Dad wants to see you in his office for a few minutes." Tessa began heading to the doors with Braeden at her side.

"I'm sorry. Just you, Tessa." Kelly shrugged her shoulders as if to say she had no idea why.

"Okay. Braeden, would you mind waiting out here with Kelly?" She gave him an odd look that he couldn't quite interpret. It appeared she didn't wish to leave him alone with Kelly.

"Nae. Go speak with yer Da, I'll be here if ye need me." Braeden noted the quizzical expression on Tessa's face as she turned and walked into John's office. He found it amusing. Kelly and Braeden had come to an understanding the previous evening when they'd been thrown together in an attempt to distract Braeden from his duties as Tessa's bodyguard. She'd been totally thrown off when Kelly's man Sean appeared at the club, but Braeden hadn't. They'd had plenty of time to speak while Tessa was busy in Danny's dressing room and Kelly had confided all about Sean and their budding relationship.

"Did you have fun last night," Kelly asked. She leaned her elbows on her desk and waited for his answer.

"Aye. I've never been to a nightclub before. 'Twas…" He hesitated, searching for the words that would describe his observations.

"Crazy? Over the top? Not anyplace you feel comfortable?" Kelly giggled.

"Aye. All of those things and more," Braeden chuckled. Kelly was a lovely lass and they found that they enjoyed each other's company. He felt a brotherly kinship with her. "And ye? Did ye have *fun*?"

"I did. You were very good company and Sean enjoyed meeting you. I think we're going to find ourselves accompanying Tessa and Danny quite a lot. Although now that she knows I'm seeing Sean she may try to find someone else for you." She smiled warmly at Braeden, reminding him that having a friend under any circumstance was a good thing, but in his case, in this place and time, it was of the utmost importance. "I hope not though, because I don't think I'll mind it at all," she teased.

Braeden cocked an eyebrow in question. "What of Sean?" He'd seen them together with his own two eyes and thought them to be in love.

Kelly giggled. "I'm just teasing you. Don't worry."

"Do ye do this teasing often?"

"Yes, I do. And I can tell it's going to be fun teasing you," she giggled.

They continued talking and laughing until the door to John's office flew open and Tessa stormed out. She stopped dead in her tracks, obviously noting the playful teasing that was going on between Braeden and Kelly.

"Are you okay?" Kelly asked.

"Fine. Braeden, my father wants to see you." Tessa stormed over to the reception area sofa and angrily plopped herself down onto it.

Braeden exchanged a questioning glance with Kelly, who merely shrugged her shoulders. With one last glance at Tessa, Braeden entered John's office, closing the door behind him.

"Braeden, it's good to see you lad." He waved Braeden over to take a seat in front of his desk. "How was your evening with Tessa and Danny?"

Braeden opened his mouth to answer, but before he could get a word out, John spoke again.

"I know this is going to be awkward for everyone concerned and I'm sure you noticed that Tessa was quite unhappy when she left my office, but I have this uncomfortable feeling that Danny is somehow mixed up with Niall Campbell. I know Niall is up to something, and if he's enlisted Danny to help him, then we're going to have big problems to deal with."

"I see why you're concerned for Tessa's safety. I didnae care for this Danny. He doesnae behave like a man in love, or a man who's to be married." Braeden stood and walked to the windows. The view took his breath away, though nothing about it was familiar to him. In Scotland he was surrounded by beauty of a different kind—green trees, lochs, the bluest of blue skies. This place. This Las Vegas was all hard stone buildings, no trees or rivers or lochs that he could see. Kelly had called it the desert. He'd never seen one in his entire life. The surrounding area was ruggedly beautiful. It was all in varying shades of brown, tan, red and gray, filled with rocks and low growing brush. There were craggy mountains rising in the distance. It was also hotter than he'd ever imagined it could be. These were all things he would have to get used to. He was a very observant man and because he was, Braeden knew that within a matter of days he'd be able to fit right in with those who lived in this time and place. He turned away from the window to address John. "I should like to meet this Niall Campbell."

"You will. I'm sure he'll be coming by often to see how business is going. I don't know if he's hoping I'll fail or if he's hoping to make me fail." John stood and joined Braeden by the window where they both looked out on the city of Las Vegas. "I'm sure this is all too fantastic for you at the moment. I'm here to help you with any questions or concerns you might have." He placed a hand on Braeden's shoulder and patted it. "Everything will work out fine."

Braeden wasn't sure if John was saying that for his benefit or his own. "I'm sure 'twill be, sir."

"None of this 'sir' stuff. Call me John. I'm happy you're here to help."

"I'd like to understand more of how I can be of service to ye. What is it ye need of me aside from guarding Tessa?" Braeden turned away from the window and faced John.

"More than I can explain to you as we stand here. It will all become clearer the longer you are here and the more you get to know about Niall, Danny and The Las Vegas Magicians and Sorcerers. Now, tell me everything that happened last night."

TESSA SAT POUTING on the sofa in the waiting room. Despite the fact that she was now very aware of being under Danny's spell, she still couldn't believe the things that were coming out of her mouth and she certainly didn't seem able to stop them. "I can't believe my father. He doesn't like Danny and he's determined to prevent me from marrying him."

"Did he say that?" Kelly asked.

"Not in so many words, but how does he expect me to have a relationship with Danny if I have to drag Braeden along with me wherever I go."

"I'm sure he's just concerned for your safety." Kelly filed some papers in her desk drawer and then stood.

"What does he think Danny's going to do to me? I wouldn't be engaged to him if I thought he was plotting and planning to do something terrible to me or my father."

"I don't know, Tessa, but I do know your father. I know him better than Danny. He would never do anything to stand in the way of your happiness. He loves you." She cast a warm smile in Tessa's direction.

"I know he loves me, which is what makes this all so perplexing." She sat silently for a few moments. She was having those confusing mixed emotions that she'd experienced a lot lately, taking her from one extreme to the other concerning Danny. "Danny was being pretty weird last night. I chalked that up to Braeden being there."

"Weird in what way," Kelly leaned back on the edge of the desk.

"I don't know. He wasn't as attentive as he usually is. He seemed distracted and was even downright rude at times. He didn't seem like he wanted to be with me." Tessa wore a sad, confused expression on her face.

"Maybe he had a bad night. Maybe things didn't go well in his show," Kelly suggested.

"He said his show was great, as usual." Tessa examined her fingernails as she spoke, her eyes wandering to the diamond Danny had given her. She wondered yet again why she couldn't seem to get a grip on what was going on in her head. Ever since she'd put that engagement ring on her finger her thinking about Danny had become clouded. "I guess no one is perfect all the time. I just hope this doesn't become a habit."

"I'm sure it won't," Kelly assured her. The door to John McTavish's office opened and both John and Braeden came out with huge smiles on their faces. As soon as Braeden saw Kelly and Tessa his smile vanished and he'd put his game face, as Tessa liked to call it, back on. He was strikingly handsome, smile or no smile, but the dark, penetrating way he looked at her made her feel all fluttery in the belly. She refused to think of the fact that Danny didn't have that effect on her. She mentally shook herself as she perused him from head to toe. She found herself doing that every time she saw him. She was developing a bad habit and it was one that she'd better shake or she was going to ruin her engagement to Danny. But isn't that what she wanted. Those thoughts began creeping back into her mind again. Hadn't she planned to break it off with Danny? Seeing Braeden brought it all back to her. Whatever spell Danny had woven had begun taking effect even when he wasn't with her, but somehow when she looked at Braeden, it weakened.

"Tessa, why don't you show Braeden around The Strip? I think it would be good for him to familiarize himself with the area."

Tessa still wasn't happy with her father, but she'd humor him. "Okay."

John came over to Tessa and pulled her into a bear hug, kissing the top of her head. "I love you very much, my darling daughter. As I've told you before, if anything ever happened to you, my life would be over."

"Dad, nothing's going to happen to me. You need to stop worrying so much." She pulled away so she could gaze into his eyes as she spoke.

"Well, I know I can stop worrying now that Braeden is here. He'll protect you with his life and I'm grateful to him for that."

Tessa rolled her eyes and shook her head. Where on earth was her father getting these crazy ideas? She'd humor him for a little while longer, but then she was going to have a serious conversation with him, because she simply couldn't live her life with Braeden MacDonald following her everywhere. "Braeden, let's go before my father decides to lock me away in a tower where no one can get to me."

John laughed out loud and turned back into his office.

"He's going to drive me crazy." Tessa stalked down the hallway away from her father's offices. "Come on. I'll get dad's limo to take us down to the south end of The Strip and we'll work our way back up. We probably won't be able to see everything today, but at least you'll be a little more familiar with everything."

Braeden grabbed Tessa's arm, effectively bringing her to a halt. "Tessa, remember yer under Danny's spell. Some things may nae make sense to ye, but remember that yer Da and I are the one's to be trusted. Remember our conversation last night as we danced?" He stared into her eyes waiting for her answer.

Memories of the previous evening crept back into her head. She was so confused. Her brain felt as if it had been cleaved in half. One side in love with Danny and the other believing what Braeden said was true. She couldn't think clearly, but on some level she understood exactly what Braeden was trying to tell her. She took a deep breath and did her best to relax. "I remember." Still, she felt an irrational anger rising within her, but she did her best to tamp it down.

Braeden didn't say a word as they continued walking. He was obviously the strong, silent type, but Tessa was determined to find out more about him. "Are you okay, Braeden? I've been so wrapped up in my own troubles, that I'd forgotten how overwhelming this all must be for you. I really want to know. Is everything okay?"

"Aye." Braeden eyed her curiously. She imagined he was having a hard time knowing which Tessa he was speaking with at any given moment and she knew exactly what he was feeling, because she felt the same way. She didn't seem to have any control over what came out of her mouth and it was frustrating her, but she had other things to take care of today, one of which was giving Braeden that tour.

"Would you like to visit the King Arthur castle down the street?"

Braeden stopped dead in his tracks. "Aye. I'd like that verra much, lass." He had a scary glint in his eye. Maybe it wasn't such a good idea after all.

"Or maybe you'd like to see one of the other casinos. There are so many beautiful ones."

"Nay. The castle. 'Tis the one I want to see first."

What had she done? This could turn out to be a very bad idea. What if he hurt someone? Braeden could end up in jail, or worse. "Braeden, I know you have this vendetta against the English, but they aren't here. I promise you. Please don't do anything we'll regret."

"I willnae do anything to embarrass ye, Tessa. I promise." Tessa watched as the muscle in his jaw twitched and belied the words that had just come from his mouth. "Shall we go then?" Braeden took her by the arm and escorted her out into the casino area.

The hotel was buzzing with customers and the casino itself was very busy for a Monday morning. Braeden continued leading her through the crowd and Tessa stopped short.

"We're going the wrong way. And you don't need to drag me along. I said I'd take you and I will. Now follow me." Tessa fixed her dress and, casting a glaring look over her shoulder at Braeden, she headed for the valet.

BRAEDEN REALIZED HE'D somehow irritated the lovely Tessa. The angry glare she'd just given him put him in his place and he followed along behind her, scanning the casino for would-be troublemakers. She may not care for it, but he was going to protect her and not just because her father had asked him to. He didnae wish to see any harm come to Tessa and he'd do whatever was necessary to protect her.

They made their way to the valet area where a car was waiting for them. Braeden waited while Tessa entered and then he joined her. These carriages were quite large and teaming with many things he'd never seen before. They were nothing like the kind he was used to, but filled with things Kelly had told him were called electronics. There was a flat screen TV and a bar, along with many other modern conveniences.

"We'll head down to the King Arthur, Sam," Tessa called to the driver.

"Yes, ma'am." Sam pulled the car out onto the busy road and they slowly made their way ever closer to the huge castle in the distance.

The King Arthur had seemed so close when Braeden had glimpsed it the other day, but now that they were traveling towards it he could see that it was actually much further away and even larger than he'd originally thought.

Tessa called out the names of the other hotels as they passed them. "That's Caesar's Palace, the Bellagio, the Cosmopolitan, New York, New York."

"All these people we see are staying in these hotels?" He tried to contain his amazement, but knew he probably wasn't doing a very good job.

"Yes. These and the others along The Strip and some off The Strip. I was reading the other day that something like forty two million people visited Las Vegas last year. I know it's always crowded with visitors, but I can't even begin to fathom that number."

"Forty two million!"

"I know. I can't imagine there were more than a million in all of Scotland in your time."

He shook his head in disbelief. As he continued gazing out the windows of the limousine, he whispered to himself, "So many people."

THEY ARRIVED AT the hotel entrance and Sam opened the door for them, Braeden exited and reached a hand out to help Tessa depart the confines of their limo. A cold, clammy feeling overcame him as he stood observing his surroundings. This was unlike any castle he'd seen in his own time. In fact, this one wasnae a castle at all. It just resembled one. He breathed a sigh of relief. Perhaps they were not the enemy after all. Perhaps it was just a hotel as John had told him. They entered the building and Braeden was immediately assailed by the sights and sounds he had come to realize were all a part of this place called Las Vegas. Tessa guided him around the casino floor, where they passed people who wore clothes that resembled medieval attire. They continued walking until at last they came to a set of double doors. Tessa opened one and Braeden was quickly at her side to take it from her, allowing her to pass through. They were in some sort of arena and, much to Braeden's delight, there were men on horseback at the center. Despite his initial thrill at seeing them, he quickly became concerned as it appeared that these men meant to behead each other as they fought with swords and dirks. There were even those participating in a joust. They stood watching for a while longer and upon further examination, Braeden realized they were only practicing. They meant each other no harm. Tessa walked him down closer to the action and to another set of doors that allowed them access to the practice field. They waited patiently for a break in the activity before opening the doors and entering.

"Tessa!" Sean called. This was Kelly's man and seeing him in the light of day, Braeden observed that he was easily of a similar height, strong and muscular with long blond hair cascading past his shoulders. He made his way toward Tessa and leaned in to kiss her cheek. "What are you doing here? I wasn't expecting a visit so soon."

"It's good to see you too, Sean," she teased. "You mentioned last night that Braeden should come by and so I thought today was as good a time as any for him to see what you all do here. I hope that's okay."

"Of course it is. Welcome to The Royal Tournament, Braeden. It's good to see you. How's my Kelly doing today?"

"Missing you, I'm sure," Braeden answered. He didn't want there to be any awkwardness between them simply because he'd been thrown together with Kelly last night.

"I don't mind hearing that at all." Sean smiled warmly at them as the others took a break and joined them. "Let me introduce you to these guys."

Sean introduced Braeden to the others and explained that they put on a nightly show here at the King Arthur. "Maybe you'd like to join us some time. I'm sure the ladies would love to see an authentic Highlander, kilt and all."

Braeden wasn't sure how to respond to that, but apparently Tessa was. "He'd love to. Wouldn't you, Braeden?"

Braeden had always been his own man. He'd always made his own decisions. Having a woman, even one as lovely as Tessa, speaking for him rankled. He hoped she wouldn't make a habit of it. Not sure how to get himself out to this mess and not wanting to embarrass Tessa by declining, he simply responded, "Aye. It would be a pleasure."

CHAPTER 9

TESSA AND SEAN were old friends, having previously dated for a while, but discovering they were much better friends, they left it at that, and now it seemed that Sean had found the woman he was meant to be with in Kelly.

"Sean, maybe you could show Braeden what you all do." Tessa had been watching Braeden as he went over to the horses and ran his hands down their sleek coats.

"Sure. Would you care to join us, Braeden? Maybe get in some swordplay?"

"Aye. I'd like that verra much." One of the others brought him a horse and he vaulted onto its bare back with ease.

Tessa couldn't take her eyes off of him. He seemed so powerful as he sat atop the black stallion they'd given him. He stroked the horse's neck and Tessa found herself imagining what it would be like to have him stroke her skin. She closed her eyes, picturing it in her mind, sending waves of desire to her heated core.

"He's a natural up there, isn't he," Sean observed, breaking her reverie.

She couldn't help her breathy response. "Yes. He is."

One of the others, who'd introduced himself as Rowan, rode up to him and handed him one of their practice swords. "Shall we?" he asked, positioning his horse next to Braeden who nodded. They turned their horses and circled in opposite directions. Braeden cantered all the way down to the other end of the arena before charging back to meet Rowan in the center. They parried back and forth, but it was obvious from the start that Braeden was a superior swordsman and horseman. He rode as one with the horse, using his legs to gently guide the huge animal without the use of reins. Tessa was mesmerized by it all. She felt like she had been transported back in time and was watching an actual battle taking place right in front of her. Of course, that was the idea of the show. It wasn't long before Braeden had knocked Rowan from atop his horse and then he quickly dismounted and they fought on foot. Rowan was obviously tiring and panting for breath, he backed away from Braeden with his hands in the air.

The others all gathered around them. "Wow! You're really good," Sean said as he clapped Braeden on the back. "I thought we'd be giving you some pointers, but you don't need them."

"Thank ye. I havenae practiced in days and I thought I might be a bit rusty." Braeden was hardly winded from the fight. The others all laughed at this statement. He handed his sword back to Sean.

"I had no idea you were an expert. Where did you learn to fight like that?" Sean appeared to be in awe of what he'd just observed.

"Back home. I've been fighting since I was a wee bairn, but I wouldnae say I was an expert. There's always room to improve."

"We should have you come down and give us some lessons. We're always open to new and authentic techniques. What do you think?" Sean turned to look at his friends, who were all smiling broadly and nodding in agreement. "You're welcome here anytime, my man. Seriously, maybe we could set something up with you for once or twice a week. Would that be alright, Tess?"

"I'm sure it would be. I'll ask my father. He's got the ultimate say so."

"Okay. Great."

"So how's everything else going down here?"

"Pretty good, although I've noticed our security guys have been extra edgy since the cleaning crew found all those clothes under one of the beds."

Tessa tipped her head and furrowed her brow. "I hadn't heard about that. What do they think happened?"

"Well, the cleaning crew was giving one of the rooms a thorough going over when one of them started pulling clothing out from under the bed. They ended up with quite a pile. It was like the guy's whole wardrobe. They reported it to their bosses and I guess it belonged to some guy who had gone missing a few days ago."

"What guy is this?"

"He was someone who had been staying at the hotel for quite some time. Longer than the usual four or five days. I think he was a friend of Niall Campbell. Anyway, Julie, one of the cleaning staff was telling me all about it. He just up and left. He didn't check out and no one knew where he'd gone. He owed quite a bit on his bill. They thought he just left unannounced, but then when they found his clothes all stuffed under the bed, it raised their suspicions. They called the police who sent some detectives down to check it out. They didn't find anything that suggested foul play, so they dropped it. Kind of weird, don't you think?"

"Very," Tessa nodded in agreement. "But then again, it is Las Vegas."

"You're right about that one," Sean said.

Braeden was now standing by Tessa's side and she could feel the heat emanating from his body. The experience of sparring with the guys had left him exhilarated and left her in awe. He seemed like a different person and Tessa was happy she'd brought him and even happier that Sean had wanted him to participate in their practice. "Are you ready to go?" Tessa asked Braeden.

"Aye. It was good to meet ye," he shook hands with the guys and then turned back to Tessa and Sean.

"We'll be in touch. You're too good not to be in our show, or at least give us a lesson or two." Sean said.

"I look forward to it."

Tessa and Braeden left the arena and Braeden's uplifted mood was clear to see. "You enjoyed that, didn't you?" She couldn't help smiling at him, he seemed so happy.

"Aye. I did."

"Do you miss it?"

"Miss what?"

"Miss being back home?"

"Aye." His mood darkened somewhat before he continued. "I wish I could have done more to save my clan. I would like to see my Grannie again and my friends, if any were left alive."

She noted the sadness in his voice and wanted more than anything to make it better for him. "I'm so sorry. This must be so strange for you. I can't even imagine what it would be like to find myself in a different time and place, wondering what had happened to my family."

"'Tis the worst feeling in the world. I hope to get back to my own time, if I can. I must avenge the deaths of my friends and family. My clan."

"Do you think you'll be able to find a way back?"

"I pray that I can."

"I'll help you if it's possible."

"Thank ye, Tessa."

THEY TOURED MORE of the hotels on The Strip, but Braeden's heart didn't seem to be in it anymore. Ever since they'd discussed his life in the past, a shroud of sadness had settled in on them. Tessa kept trying to lighten the mood, but nothing she did seemed to help. *Lesson learned, don't bring up the past.*

The rest of the day was spent back at The Albannach and for once, Tessa didn't mind having Braeden tagging along. He'd actually saved her from being manhandled by a drunken customer near the slot machines. He was surprisingly gentle with the man, spinning him away from Tessa and handing him off to another security member. Tessa felt her admiration for Braeden growing. There was something about him that, over the few days she'd known him, had affected her deeply. She still didn't think she needed a bodyguard, but if she had to have one, she was glad it was Braeden. All of her arguing and complaining about it was futile. He was only doing his job and if she was going to be upset with anyone, it should be her father… and perhaps Danny. She hadn't heard from him all day. Was he avoiding her? She'd texted him several times throughout the day, but he hadn't answered. She tried calling, but again no response. It was very unlike him, but in reality, this had been coming on for a while now. It seemed that as soon as Danny got Tessa to say yes, his whole persona changed. He wasn't as attentive, he wasn't as affectionate and he seemed to grow more and more distant with each passing day. She'd already decided she couldn't marry him, but she had to tell him and she wanted to do it in person. She fidgeted with her engagement ring, feeling like she wanted to remove it, but every time she tried, it refused to budge. It fit her perfectly when Danny placed it on her finger and she was pretty sure her fingers hadn't grown. She continued trying to remove it, but had no luck. Tessa didn't realize that the whole while she'd been thinking about Danny and her ring, she'd been frowning, but obviously Braeden had noticed.

"Is all well with ye, Tessa? Ye seem quite bothered."

"I'm okay. I was just thinking." She made a conscious effort to relax her face.

"About what?"

"About Danny."

"Have ye now?"

"I've been pretty confused over the past few days. At first I was ecstatic to be engaged to Danny and I felt very in love." Tessa checked Braeden for his reaction, but true to his nature, he remained somewhat stoic. "Then things started getting weird. You and I have talked about it." She checked in with him again and this time he nodded. "So I want to tell him I can't marry him. I need to do it soon because it's driving me crazy thinking about it, but I can't get a hold of him. He seems to have dropped off the face of the earth."

"I ken ye wish to tell him face-to-face. How will ye find him?"

"I don't know. Maybe I should just leave well enough alone."

"What does that mean?"

"Nothing. It's just a saying. I'm going to keep trying to get in touch with him. When I do, I'll suggest we all go out again tonight. Then if you'll give me a few minutes alone with him, I'll tell him."

Braeden cocked a brow in her direction.

"I know you're supposed to go everywhere with me, but all I need is a few minutes alone with him so I can tell him I can't marry him and then maybe get some answers about his weird behavior."

"I'll be close by, but I believe ye should avoid discussing his behavior of late. Just call off yer engagement and then we'll get out of there. I cannae allow any harm to come to ye."

Tessa smiled brightly at him as a secret thrill ran through her at the thought of Braeden wanting to protect her, even though she still didn't believe Danny would harm her. "Thank you, Braeden. I appreciate it. Maybe you should ask Kelly to join us." A little bit of jealousy tugged at Tessa's heart as she made that suggestion, even though she knew Kelly and Sean were dating.

"Aye. I will. As soon as we get back." He gave her that seldom seen smile. The smile she coveted. The smile she didn't want him to share with anyone but her.

"TESSA NEEDS US again tonight," Braeden said. "Would ye join me on a date?"

"I will if we can call it something other than a date. I do have a man of my own, you know."

"Aye. My apologies to Sean. He's a verra lucky man. I dinnae wish to take ye away from him, but Tessa would feel better if you come with us."

"Tessa and Sean were an item for a little while last year and she didn't know I've been seeing him. I wasn't sure how she'd react when she found out, but things went pretty well last night, wouldn't you say?"

"Aye. They are friends now?"

"Yeah. That's kind of nice. I'm not friends with any of my exes." She wrinkled her nose, showing Braeden how she felt about that idea.

Braeden thought he was really going to have to learn what some of these modern words meant. Things were different here, but not that much different when it came to the way people behaved when they were in love or out of it.

"I really should run this by Sean first. I'm feeling like he could be the one and I don't want to screw it up."

"Ye dinnae wish to upset him because ye wish to have a future to-gether?" Her words were confusing to him, so he repeated what he thought she meant.

"Right."

"I saw Sean today. Tessa took me to the castle, but 'tis nae a real castle. I dinnae ken why they have need of knights."

"It's a show. The Royal Tournament. Hundreds of people come in every night to eat and drink as if they were back in Medieval times. Sean and the guys entertain them. They pretend to be real knights waging a battle for the hand of a royal princess."

Braeden noted that Kelly was looking at him rather oddly and thought it best to change the subject. "I sparred with Rowan today. He was verra good, but he could be better."

"I take that to mean you beat him." She was a charming lass and her teasing grin warmed Braeden's heart.

"Aye. I did just that," Braeden bragged.

"I don't know much about you, Braeden, but it's almost as if you're from a different time. The way you speak and act. Call me crazy, but I'd almost believe you were."

"Mayhap I am, m'lady." He'd tell her at some point, but for now he simply used her own teasing tactics against her.

Kelly wrinkled her nose at him, signaling her disbelief. "I should get back to work. I've got a bunch of appointments I need to schedule for John."

"Good. I'll see you this evening then." Braeden winked at Kelly and turned back down the hallway. Tessa was with her father and he'd assured Braeden that he'd see to it that she got back to their apartments without incident.

Walking through the casino he was struck once again by all the sights and sounds constantly assailing his senses. He shook his head and walked as quickly as he could to the doors that led to the McTavish private quarters. He'd get used to it someday, he told him-self, but for now he would do his best to appear unaffected by it all.

CHAPTER 10

"I GUESS WE'RE NOT going anywhere tonight. I still haven't been able to get a hold of Danny. I wonder where he could be." Tessa walked into the living room of the McTavish residence carrying a large bowl filled with a food Braeden didn't recognize. "You should probably let Kelly know we're not going out."

"I told her earlier that ye hadnae heard from Danny and that if ye did I would contact her."

"Oh, good, so she's not sitting around waiting for us then." Tessa plopped herself on the sofa next to Braeden and offered him the bowl.

"What's this?" he asked, taking it from her.

"Popcorn. I thought we'd watch a movie or something and just hang out here tonight. See, I got all comfy in my pajamas." She hopped up again and went to the bar where she retrieved two bottles, bringing them back to the sofa. "Beer for you and cider for me."

After settling the bowl of popcorn in his lap, he took the icy cold bottle of beer from Tessa and brought it to his lips.

"Wait. We should make a toast." Tessa held her bottle up to his.

"What will we toast?" he asked.

"We'll toast to another successful day at The Albannach." She clinked her bottle up against his and took a sip.

Braeden did the same and then tentatively took a piece of popcorn and put it in his mouth.

"What do you think?" Tessa asked, watching him eat.

"Most unusual, but I like it." He dipped his hand in the bowl and took more.

"I knew you'd like it." She helped herself to the popcorn. "Where's Da?"

"He said he was quite tired and he was going to bed."

"He's been working so hard. He really needs his rest."

"Aye."

"I guess it's just you and me then. I'll find us a movie to watch." She picked up another one of those objects that had no name that he knew of. "This is the remote control. Let me show you how it works." She explained how to turn the television on and off, how to control the sound and how to change the channels.

Braeden was suitably confused by all the new words, but he did his best to memorize the workings of this 'remote control.' Finding a movie she thought he'd like, Tessa got everything set and the television came to life.

He was enjoying this time alone with Tessa. She sat next to him, but far enough away that they weren't touching. He wished there was a way to get her to move closer, but he couldn't think of anything he could do that wouldn't be obvious. He'd already thrown his arm over the back of the sofa, but that didn't really help.

Tessa stood, taking the empty popcorn bowl and bottles. "Is there anything else you want?" she asked as she headed for the kitchen.

He wanted to say, *Aye! I want ye here in me arms. I wish to kiss ye and feel yer ruby lips on me. I want to carry ye up those stairs to me room and make love to ye.* But instead he said, "Nae."

ॐ

TESSA PUT EVERYTHING away in the kitchen and then headed back to Braeden. She had him all to herself and she couldn't figure out how she could get his hands on her. She didn't want to embarrass herself. She was pretty sure he wanted her, but she'd prefer it if he made the first move, just to be sure.

Returning to the sofa she decided to get more comfortable. She fluffed up the pillows and laid down, stretching her legs so that her feet landed in Braeden's lap. That wasn't too forward, was it?

"Oh, I'm sorry." She moved her feet, but before she got too far, Braeden grabbed them and placed them back in his lap.

"'Tis fine." He held her feet in his large hands and gently massaged them.

"Mmm… Oh, that feels so good. My feet were killing me from wearing high heels all day. Thank you." She got what she wanted. His hands were definitely on her. Now if she could get him to work his way up from her feet, she'd be a happy camper.

His deep, dark seductive eyes were aimed right at her and she thought for one brief moment that he might grant her wish, but then he looked away and back to the movie. He kept rubbing her feet and

Tessa decided it was best to just relax and enjoy it. Her feet seemed to have a direct connection to her womanly center and as she closed her eyes enjoying the sensation all she could think about was Braeden MacDonald's hands moving up her legs, into her pajamas and…

"Tessa," Braeden called to her. "Are ye asleep, lass?"

Had she fallen asleep? If so, that was quite the dream she was having. "I'm sorry. I guess I'm really tired. The foot massage relaxed me so much I couldn't keep my eyes open. I didn't say anything, did I?" She occasionally talked in her sleep and she'd be mortified if she'd done so just now.

"Nae. Ye looked so peaceful that I hated to wake ye, but wouldnae ye be more comfortable up in your own bed?"

"You know, I probably would be." Tessa reluctantly removed her feet from his hands and swinging her legs off of the sofa, stood. "Good night."

"I'll escort ye to yer room." Braeden stood and was at her side in a flash.

"Okay, but you really don't have to." *Unless you want to join me,* she thought. She turned off the television and the lights.

"I'll come with ye." Braeden put an arm around her shoulders and guided her to the stairs.

What did he mean by that? Did he mean he was going to bed with her or he was going to bed in his own room. All she knew was if he didn't stop touching her, she wasn't going to be responsible for what was going to happen.

At the top of the stairs he guided her to her door and then stood facing her. He touched the tip of her nose with his finger and with a look of regret on his handsome face, turned towards his own room. She stood there not knowing what to do next. She wanted to call him back, but realized she really shouldn't. Instead, she opened her bedroom door and went in arguing with herself all the way.

HIS ROOM SEEMED cold and lonely. Braeden pulled back the bed covers, removed his kilt and climbed in. He would have much preferred Tessa's bed, but it wouldnae be right to take advantage of the situation. He could see from the way she licked her lips and played with her hair that she would have liked him to join her, but he couldn't betray John's trust. This was going to be one torturous lesson in self control for Braeden. When she'd put her feet in his lap, he had all he could do to restrain himself. Massaging her feet had been torture. He wanted to do so much more and then when she fell asleep and began talking, he couldn't believe his ears. He'd lied and told her she hadn't said a word, because if she'd known, she 'd likely be embarrassed and would surely never cast a glance his way again. He knew now, she wanted him and he'd have her, but only when the time was right.

Sleeping wouldn't be easy for him, but he closed his eyes and dreamed an angel named Tessa granted his wish.

FURTHER DOWN THE Strip, Danny Madden was finished with his show and back in his dressing room. If he thought he could have gotten away with it, he would have missed the show altogether and headed out of town sooner, but he knew there were eyes on him almost always. Missing the show was a risk that he simply couldn't afford. He'd also avoided Tessa all day. She'd been calling and leaving messages since this morning, but it was best that he keep her in the dark for now. She'd find out soon enough what was going on and he hoped she'd understand.

He grabbed his bag, hurrying from his dressing room and to his car. He had to get to the airport. His flight was leaving in less than an hour. He only hoped he'd make it on time.

CHAPTER *11*

THE SOUND OF Tessa's sobbing had Braeden bolting out of his own room and into hers to see what was wrong.

"Tessa, are ye well?" The sight of her sitting on the edge of her bed in tears tore at his heart.

"I'll be fine," she sniffled and coughed. "I'm just upset and I'm not even sure why."

"Aye. I have eyes to see that ye are. Would ye like to tell me what has happened?"

Braeden assumed it must be something to do with her father. "It's Danny. He's called off our engagement."

"Is that nae what ye wished, lass?" Concern for Tessa overrode his secret elation at this news.

"It is. I was so concerned about telling him in person and then he goes and does it by text. I know I shouldn't be upset about this, but it's, it's... I can't explain it."

"What's happened to change his mind?" Braeden was hoping it might shed some light on John's problems with Niall.

"I don't know. He admitted he hadn't been himself lately, but that was all he said, other than that he didn't want to marry me. He apologized and that was it. I texted him back and he didn't answer, so that's why I didn't hear from him yesterday."

"Texted?" Braeden wasn't sure what that meant. He'd heard her use the term several times and hoped he'd figure it out on his own, but to this point he still had no idea what she was speaking of.

"On my phone. You've seen me texting people." Tessa held up her phone to show him what she meant. She grabbed a tissue and wiped her eyes.

"Why are ye upset, lass. Ye didnae love him, remember?"

"I know, but reading his text just now, I had the strangest reaction.

I was overjoyed, but I couldn't control my tears."

"Are ye sure ye didnae love him?" He had to be sure.

"I said I didn't," Tessa snapped.

"I don't know ye verra well, Tessa and I'd only just met Danny, and so I've nae been privy to your relationship with him. In my time, women dinnae always marry men because they love them. It is sometimes out of necessity. I apologize if I upset ye."

Tessa sat quietly. She was obviously trying to get herself under control. "It's okay. I shouldn't have snapped at you like that. I don't know what's wrong with me." She flung her arm in the air, gesturing her exasperation, and her engagement ring went flying.

Both Braeden and Tessa watched as it sailed through the air and then vanished. They exchanged confused glances.

"Did you see that?" Tessa asked.

"Where did it go?" Braeden stood and searched the floor beneath the spot where it had last been visible. "'Tis nae here."

"I've been trying to get that damn ring off for days now and it wouldn't budge. Do you think it was what held the spell Danny was using to keep me in check?" Her eyes searched his face as if the answer she sought might be found there.

Braeden went and sat next to Tessa on the bed, wrapping one strong arm around her shoulders, pulling her in so that her wet cheek rested on his chest. "I'm sorry, Tessa. If I can help in any way, I will."

Tessa sank into him and much to his surprise she put her arm around his waist. A jolt of wanting ran through him. His attraction to Tessa had been apparent to him from the moment he met her, but until this very moment he thought she belonged to another and it wouldnae be honorable to steal another man's woman. This was nae the time for it, but all he could think of was what it might be like to lift her chin, look in her eyes and kiss her sweet lips. He knew he should move away from her, but he didnae wish to disturb her. She'd made herself quite at home in his embrace and he wasnae going to deny that he was enjoying it.

"Tessa!" John McTavish was calling to his daughter from the bottom of the stairs. "I'll go speak with him," Braeden offered.

Tessa reluctantly loosened her grip on him and wiped her eyes. "No. I'll go. Dad was right about Danny and I should be the one to tell him."

Standing, Braeden held out a hand to Tessa, which she took without hesitation. He pulled her up from the bed and wiped one final tear from her cheek with his thumb and, planting a soft kiss on her forehead, guided her down the stairs to her father.

৯৩

To TESSA'S EYES, her father appeared quite sad. It was almost as if he knew what had happened.

"Tessa, please come in the living room with me and sit down for a minute. I have some news to share with you."

"Braeden, please join us." John motioned with his head for Braeden to sit beside Tessa.

John pulled the ottoman over and sitting in front of her, took her hands.

"What's wrong, Da? Did someone die?" Tessa's confused expression and John's serious one had Braeden on edge.

"Sweetheart, I don't know how to tell you this, but Danny's dead." John clutched Tessa's hand even tighter and Braeden offered support by moving closer and placing a protective arm around her shoulder.

"The police haven't ruled out foul play. They're investigating right now and hope to have more information for us later today. I'm so sorry. I didn't like or trust, Danny, but I know you loved him and I've dreaded telling you."

To Braeden's surprise, Tessa didn't break down. Instead she sat up straight and tall, with both of her hands clasping her father's. "Dad, there's something you should know. I don't think I ever really loved Danny. I think he was continuously casting a spell on me that made me *think* I loved him. I wanted to tell him I couldn't marry him, but every time I tried it was as if the words lodged in my throat." She appeared thoughtful before she spoke again. "Danny broke off our engagement by text this morning sometime, but for some reason it just appeared on my phone a few minutes ago."

"I got the call after you went up to your room. What an odd coincidence. I wonder if there's a connection." John had risen and was pacing back and forth in front of Braeden and Tessa.

"It is strange. I should speak with the police about it. They'll need that information." Tessa watched as her father paced. "Dad, everything's going to be okay, isn't it?"

John stopped his pacing and stood gazing at the front door as if he was planning to leave. "For now, you should take it easy. I'll contact the police and see if they can send someone around to speak with you."

"I need to keep busy, Dad. I can't just sit here," Tessa protested.

The phone rang and John left Tessa to answer it. "Yes. Yes. I see. Did they catch them? All right, let me know when you hear." He put the phone down and turned back to Tessa and Braeden. "That was

Margaret Camden. Someone tried to remotely open our vault. Luckily they failed."

"Why would someone do that? If they opened the vault remotely, it wouldn't do them any good, especially if they were trying to steal money from the casino. Someone would have to be here to go in once the vault was opened." Tessa was obviously trying to process everything that was going on here today. "And how on earth do you remotely open a safe?"

"Those are all good questions. Margaret says that when one of the cashier crew went to open the safe a short while ago, the tumblers were all moving. She called security and they all stood there watching as the dials moved back and forth. I'm assuming whoever did this was trying to decipher the code to get in. Hopefully, they haven't figured it out."

"We can change the combination, but Da, I'm still not understanding. Who could do something like that?"

"I believe our friends at the Las Vegas Magick and Sorcery Society might have the answer to that question. I've been receiving information from a man I hired to infiltrate the Society, but I haven't heard from him since the day of the Grand Opening."

"Was that the man I saw you talking with? You seemed angry about something. I meant to ask you about it, but in all the excitement of opening day I forgot."

"Yes. His name is Alfred Winchester. He was telling me that Niall was meeting with someone who works here at the hotel. He wasn't sure who it was, but he thought he was close to figuring it out."

"Dad, was this man staying at The King Arthur?" Tessa had a bad feeling about this.

"He was. Why do you ask?"

"Braeden and I were down there yesterday and Sean told us that some man affiliated with Niall Campbell had up and left without a word. He didn't even take his clothes with him. They were found under the hotel room bed." Tessa observed her father's reaction to this information. He sat silently for a moment, obviously processing what he'd just been told.

"Braeden, I need you to stay with Tessa. Never leave her side. We've got to get to the bottom of this before they succeed in getting into the safe. If they do, we'll be out of business." John plunked himself down on the edge of the sofa.

The three of them sat and stared at each other, not knowing quite what to do under the circumstances. John suddenly rose to his feet. "I'm calling Niall Campbell. I'm going to schedule a meeting with him. Tessa and Braeden, I'd like you there. If he's behind this, we'll find out—one way or the other."

"MY FATHER'S CALLING Niall, right now. This is all so weird." Tessa and Braeden were seated in John's outer office.

"Are you okay?" Kelly asked.

"I have to be. I can't be a sobbing mess in the middle of what's going on. I want to be helpful, if I can." Tessa hadn't shed another tear since leaving their residence with Braeden and her father. It was as if whatever spell she'd been under had been lifted and she could clearly see she'd had no feelings for Danny whatsoever.

"Well, if you need anything, I'm here for you."

"I know, Kelly. I appreciate your friendship so much."

"The feeling's mutual." Kelly came around her desk and wrapped her arms around Tessa, giving her a warm hug.

The two women stood that way for a while before pulling away. Tessa had tears in her eyes, not tears of sadness, but tears that said how much Kelly's friendship meant to her. "Thanks, sweetie."

The doors to John's office opened and he came out. "Niall will be joining us shortly. He seemed shocked to hear about Danny. I thought the two might be connected somehow, but he seemed genuinely surprised to hear it."

"Seeing him in person will make it easier to see if he's telling the truth or lying," Tessa offered.

"Why don't you two go check in with Margaret about the safe and I'll have Kelly find you when Niall arrives."

John returned to his office, while Tessa and Braeden headed off to the casino floor and the cashier's booth. They barely spoke as they perused the gaming tables, the slots and the bars. There were no obvious problems and the security team was well equipped to handle anything that might arise. There were, of course, the occasional shouts of people winning or of those who'd had too much to drink and who were beginning to become a nuisance, but escorting the inebriated from the building or back to their rooms had become routine.

They passed through the ornate doors that only allowed access to those whose thumbprints matched the keypad. The symbol of the Celtic Tree of Life was significant to Tessa and John, which is why she'd chosen it for the door to the cashier's room and the safe. The symbolism of the tree was appropriate in its use throughout the hotel, but even more so here. It was considered a door to another realm. When people passed through the doors here at The Albannach, the hope was that they would leave their world behind, entering this new world created by John and Tessa. Here it led to the hotel safe and passage was dependent on one proving they belonged there. Braeden and Tessa passed through and were greeted by Margaret who wore a worried expression on her face.

"Tell me what happened," Tessa said.

"Everything was going pretty smoothly as it usually does, when Kenneth called out to me that the tumblers on the vault were spinning. I ran over and couldn't believe my eyes. They were moving all by themselves. How is that even possible?" Margaret appeared puzzled by what had happened and who could blame her.

"I'm not sure. We've got the safe company stopping by to take a look at everything, just to be sure it wasn't some sort of malfunction. I think it would be a good idea to change the passcode, in case by some strange chance it was remotely affected." Tessa walked to the safe and examined it closely. She had no idea what she might be looking for, but felt that if something was wrong it was possible she could spot it. After a few minutes of spinning the tumblers and checking the seal of the door, she gave up.

"I'm baffled. This is the craziest thing I've ever heard of."

"I'm with you there," Margaret said.

"We're adding extra security outside of this room. No one will be able to enter without going through them first."

Braeden stood motionless as a statue. He was on high alert from the looks of him. Tessa was happy he was there to help them. Her father had explained to her that Braeden was a seasoned warrior back in his own time and that he would protect her with his life if necessary. She hoped it wouldn't come to that. Having him on her side during this difficult time would be a blessing.

Margaret was unaware of the news about Danny, so Tessa decided to tell her. "I've had some bad news this morning. Danny Madden's dead."

"What? How?" Margaret seemed shocked by this news and why wouldn't she be. Tessa stuffed any feelings she had about Danny—good, bad or indifferent—to the back of her mind. She was still processing everything, but she refused to let that get in the way of her doing her job. There was nothing she could've done and nothing she could do now to save Danny. Protecting everything her father had worked so hard to attain was the priority first and foremost as far as she was concerned.

"I'm so sorry, Tessa. If there's anything at all that I can do to help, please let me know."

"Thanks, but I don't think there's much anyone can do. We're waiting to hear from the police about the cause of death. Until we do, we just have to wait and concentrate our efforts on keeping things here at the casino safe."

"Agreed. Your father has doubled security here and around the casino, so if anyone tries anything, we should be able to stop them, hopefully before they pull anything off." She glanced at Braeden. "And I'm happy to see that you have your own personal bodyguard, Tessa. We wouldn't want anything to happen to you."

Tessa smiled as best she could. "It looks like you've got things under control here, so we'll let you get back to work."

As they exited the room, Braeden broke his silence. "How well do ye know this woman?"

"Why?"

"Me gut is telling me that we need to keep an eye on her. Mayhap we should speak with Kenneth. He saw the same thing Margaret saw, didnae he?"

"You're right. I wish I'd thought of that when I was in there. She pulled out her cell phone and put it to her ear and waited a moment before speaking. "Margaret is Kenneth there?"

"Ok. No problem. I'll speak with him later then." Tessa turned back to Braeden, sliding her cell phone into her back pocket. "She said he went home. He had the early shift and it was over. Do you think it would be a good idea to go see him there?"

"Aye, but how will we find him?"

"Don't worry. We'll go to personnel. They'll have his address. Hopefully he's at home."

They headed to the personnel office where they gathered the information they needed and then got Tessa's car and driver from the valet.

"Baltimore Street." Tessa handed him the address she'd jotted down. Sam glanced down at the address. "You sure you want to go there?"

"Yes. There's someone we need to speak with at that address."

Sam appeared apprehensive as the car pulled away from the hotel and headed for the freeway, where they went a few miles before exiting in a rather unsavory part of town.

"I'm not so sure about this, Miss McTavish. This is a pretty bad neighborhood." Sam was gripping the steering wheel so tightly his knuckles were turning white.

"Dinnae fear, Sam. I'm with ye." Braeden sounded so proud and sure of himself that Tessa had to hide her chuckle.

They pulled into a parking lot in front of a run-down apartment complex. Young men were lounging around on the cars in the lot and on the stairs that led up to the second floor apartments.

"I'll stay here with the car, Miss McTavish." Sam inclined his head towards a group that were eyeing the car with interest.

"Thanks. Stay inside with the doors locked and if there's any trouble, honk the horn. Be safe." Tessa glanced around and for the first time questioned her decision to come looking for Kenneth. She could have waited until the next day, but something about today's incidents made it seem urgent that she speak with him. "Come on, Braeden. I believe his apartment is on the second floor."

They stepped from the car and the group of men began laughing and cat-calling Braeden, who wore his kilt.

"Hey, what're you two ladies doing here?" One particularly cocky guy stood in their way as they walked towards the stairs. He checked back with the others who were all laughing and now whistling at Braeden, crowding around in an effort to scare them. "Well don't you look pretty in your skirt." He flicked at the hem with his fingers and then got right in front of Braeden with his arms folded, as if to keep them from proceeding.

Braeden put a protective arm around Tessa and gave them a menacing glare that silenced them. He pushed the leader out of the way and followed Tessa as she headed towards the stairs and another group of younger men who sat unmoving, ogling her as she approached. Once they noted Braeden behind her, they parted to allow them access to the stairs. They climbed to the second floor and then searched until they found apartment 218. Tessa knocked, but there was no answer. She knocked again and still nothing. They were about to walk away when the door finally opened to reveal a rather disheveled woman with three small children hiding behind her.

"Yes." Her eyes were filled with suspicion as she glanced from Braeden to Tessa. "What do you want?"

"We're looking for Kenneth Carra," Tessa stated.

"He's not here. What do you want him for?"

"He works at The Albannach Hotel for my father and I wanted to ask him a few questions."

"He's not here," she said again.

"Do you know where he is or when he might be back?"

"No. He's usually home by now."

"Does he ever go anywhere else before coming home?"

"No. He comes right home. I have to get to work and someone has to be here with the kids." Three sets of eyes peered out from behind her. They were staring up at Braeden who winked at them, causing them to squeeze past their mother, who tried her best to stop them, but they were faster than she was.

"Why are you wearing a skirt?" the oldest boy asked.

"'Tis nae a skirt, young lad. 'Tis a kilt." Braeden ruffled the boy's hair. "What be yer name?"

The boy looked to his mother and then back to Braeden. "Brandon."

"Brandon. What a coincidence! Mine is Braeden. I'm please to meet ye."

Braeden held his hand out and the boy took it, shaking it vigorously. "Yer a strong one, arenae ye?"

"You talk funny," said the girl, who appeared to be the middle child.

"Aye. I do. Where I'm from everyone talks this way." He smiled brightly at this little one, putting her at ease. She broke into a grin, that showed she was missing some teeth. "Where are yer teeth, lass?"

"They fell out. The tooth fairy took them."

"Did she now?"

"She gave me some money."

"Was it enough, do ye think?"

She shrugged her shoulders and shyly looked down at her shoes.

The youngest boy, who couldn't have been more than two had wrapped an arm around Braeden's leg and was tugging on this kilt. He picked the boy up in his arms. "And who have we here?"

"That's my brother," the oldest boy said. "His name is James. My sister's name is Hayden."

"I'm pleased to meet ye." Braeden handed James back to his mother.

"We won't keep you any longer, Mrs. Carra. When you see him can you have him call me?" Tessa handed the woman her business card, which she perused.

"Is he in trouble?" She appeared worried.

"No. Not at all." Tessa reassured her with a warm smile. "I just need-ed to talk with him."

"I'll let him know you stopped by." She closed the door and left them standing there.

"I wonder why Kenneth lives in a place like this," Tessa said. "He makes good money working at The Albannach. He could surely afford better." She hadn't met Kenneth prior to this, but she'd have to ask Margaret about him. She hated to see those three little darlings grow-ing up surrounded by the gang from the parking lot.

By the time they got back downstairs, the car was surrounded by young men and Sam, who sat defiantly, hands clutching the steering wheel, was eyeing them warily.

"What do ye think yer up to here?" Braeden stood to his full height and pulled his sword from its sheath. Brandishing it with both hands, he took a threatening stance facing them.

"Nothing. We ain't doing nothing." The obvious leader said.

"Then would ye mind doing nothing over there?" Braeden swung his sword in the direction he wanted them to go and they ran. He smiled broadly and glanced the driver's way. Sam was giving him a thumb's up for his efforts as he unlocked the door for them to get in. Braeden waited for Tessa to get in and then took one final glance back at the would-be thugs before joining her.

"Thanks, man. I was starting to get worried about what they might do." Sam relaxed in the driver's seat.

"'Twas nothing."

Tessa was very impressed and said so. "That wasn't *nothing*. You scared the living daylights out of them. It's a good thing we came back when we did and a good thing you always have that sword with you. Are you okay, Sam?"

"I'm fine now. Where to? I assume you want to get out of here. I know I'd like to and the sooner the better."

"Back to the casino please."

"You got it."

Braeden sat silently next to her. She could feel his tension release after a few moments in the car. "I wonder where Kenneth could be. I would have suggested we wait for him there, but I don't think that would have been the safest plan."

"Ye can speak with him when he comes back to work."

"I'll check the schedule when we get back to see when he works next."

Braeden nodded at this and gazed out the window. She wondered what he must be thinking. Tessa tried to put herself in his shoes, imagining she was seeing and experiencing all of this for the first time. She had to admit it was overwhelming to say the least. She felt a growing fondness for Braeden. Even though she hadn't known him for long, she could tell he was a good man. She would be safe with him. A momentary vision of Danny came to mind and she gave her relationship with him some thought. She'd placed it all at the back of her mind in order to make it through the day, but here, riding silently back to the hotel, she wondered about him. The more she thought about it, the more she knew he hadn't loved her at all. The question was, why had he asked her to marry him? The next question was, why had she agreed? She knew the answer to that was as far fetched and complicated as it seemed. He'd cast a spell on her. The more she thought about their time together, the more it made perfect sense and the more she felt like a fool for not knowing and stopping it sooner. He'd never really felt anything for her. He'd been doing his job and that job was as fiancé to Tessa McTavish.

"Are ye well, Tessa?" Braeden asked, apparently noting the scowl on her face. "I will be. Just processing everything that's happened today."

Braeden took her hand and warmth rushed up her arm. "I ken ye've heard this much today, but I truly mean it. I'm here fer ye."

"I know, Braeden, and I'm happy you are." She smiled warmly at him. She could tell that even though he was doing his job as her bodyguard, that he would do it even if it weren't his job. He was simply that kind of man. Her father had been wise to employ him and she considered herself lucky that he had.

BRAEDEN WAS WORRIED for Tessa and for John. Something was wrong. He could feel it. It wasn't just all of the things that had occurred that day. There was a feeling in the air and more importantly, his watch had been vibrating on and off all day. He took it from his sporran and held it in his hand. He wondered what would happen if he wished himself back to his own time. As quickly as he had the thought, he pushed it aside. There was no way he was going to leave Tessa and John in their hour of need. He'd left his own time before he had been able to help his clan defeat the Campbells, but he wasn't about to abandon anyone here in this time, no matter what may occur.

Tessa was safely in her bedroom. After the stressful day she had, Braeden hoped she was sleeping peacefully and dreamlessly. She was exhausted and needed to rest. For his part, he sat on the bed in his room trying to remember how to use the remote control Tessa had given him. She'd explained last night that it would allow him to watch the shiny, black rectangle placed just above the dresser. He'd seen them throughout the casino and was curious about them. He pushed the button Tessa told him would turn the thing on and it came to life. He watched in amazement as a man and a woman explained to him all of the things he could see and do at the casino. He watched this for a while and then it repeated itself. He gazed at the remote control and began pushing buttons. The scenes on the black object began flashing on and off, until he landed on one where a woman was explaining how to cook. He was fascinated and watched with wonder. His tummy began to growl and his mouth began to water at the sight of such delicious food. Braeden turned the TV off and headed downstairs to the kitchen, where he hoped to find something to sate his hunger.

Tessa had explained to him that they didn't keep much food stocked because they could eat anywhere they wanted in the hotel, so he wasn't expecting much. When he walked into the room, he was surprised to see John sitting on a stool eating.

"Braeden! Good to see you. You must be hungry. Sit. Sit. I'll get you something to eat."

"Thank ye, sir. I'm verra hungry."

"I would imagine you are. A man of your size needs many calories to make it through the day and spending time with Tessa, who eats like a bird, I'm not surprised at all that you are famished."

John scurried around the counter to the stove and using the same frying pan he had obviously just used, turned on the flame. Braeden couldn't believe his eyes. He hadn't had to work at all to get the fire started. This world was full of many wonders. Would he ever see them all? John opened another door and a light came on. Cold air also rushed out.

"What is that?" Braeden questioned.

"It called a refrigerator. It keeps food and drinks cold, so they don't go bad."

Braeden nodded his head as if he understood what John was talking about, but obviously John was on to him. He began explaining everything in the kitchen to Braeden. The stove, the refrigerator, the microwave, the dishwasher. All were amazing inventions that would have made life so much easier back in his time. What would they do all day if they didn't have to do all of the labor involved with cooking and feeding others? He couldn't even fathom it, but thought his grandmother would love it all.

"The hotel buffet has a much larger version of this kitchen. There are also kitchens in each of the hotel restaurants. You should have Tessa show them to you. They are quite a bit different than this one." When he was finished with what he was doing, John placed a plate, napkins and utensils in front of Braeden. He then slipped some eggs from the pan directly onto the plate. This was followed by toasted bread, butter and jam. "Eat up, lad. You're going to need your strength."

Braeden wondered what he meant by that. He put a forkful of food in his mouth. "This is verra good, sir."

"What did I tell you about calling me sir. It's John."

"John." Braeden might never get used to calling him John. He was the man he worked for and he deserved respect, but as he'd already noted, things were different in this time period.

"Braeden, I believe we are merely at the beginning stages of what is to come. Someone is going to try to rob the hotel. They made that obvious this morning when they were playing about with the tumblers. I also believe that whoever is the mastermind of this plot also killed Danny."

The food on his plate disappeared quickly and John busily made him more. "So, how's my little girl?"

"Tessa?" Braeden wasn't sure if he'd consider Tessa a little girl, so he wanted to clarify that with John.

"Yes. She's my one and only. I worry about her, but then what parent doesn't worry about their children."

Braeden quietly listened as John talked more about Tessa.

"She's a very capable young lady and I have no doubt she'll handle all this business with Danny without issue."

"We went to speak with Kenneth today." Braeden muttered between mouthfuls of food.

"Who's Kenneth?"

"I'm sorry. I thought ye'd know him, but when I think on it, how could ye know the names of every man and woman working here."

"I'd like to and I will eventually, but it is only our first week open. Give me some time." John chuckled.

"Kenneth was there when the safe tumblers were turning today."

"Oh, yes. He works with Margaret. What did he say?"

"We couldnae find him. I'm worried that something has happened to him."

"Why are you worried, Braeden? Tell me about it."

"Whoever is behind this mayhap didnae want anyone to know what they were up to. He saw it and they may fear he'd tell someone."

"But we know about it. Margaret told us. Do you think she may be in danger as well?"

"I'm nae certain, but do ye think Margaret may have something to do with it?"

John thought about this for a while before answering. "That's a good question. I've known Margaret for years. We've worked together before at some other casinos on The Strip. I would never have suspected her of doing something like that. She was always very honest, which is why I hired her."

"We should keep watch on her either way. If she's had no hand in it then she may verra well need our protection."

"Good call, Braeden. You're going to be invaluable to me." He clapped him on the back. "How's the food?"

"Verra good." He gulped down some water. "Better than at the restaurants." Braeden missed his Grannie's cooking and sitting here with John in this verra fancy kitchen somehow brought him back home, if only in his mind. He missed his Grannie more than he could express.

John broke into a wide grin. "I'm pleased to hear it. I used to work as a cook for a while. I'm sure you know I tried to work every job I possibly could before opening The Albannach. I have to say that by far, my favorite was being a line cook. I've always preferred to make my own meals, but since The Albannach has opened I don't have the time."

"I don't see how ye do it, John. So many people and such a large castle. Do ye ever sleep?"

"I do and that's what I'm going to do now. Good night, Braeden."

"Good night, John."

He sat in the kitchen and for the first time since being brought to Las Vegas, he felt completely alone. It wasn't an unfamiliar feeling to him. He'd been alone before in his life, but he always knew the people he loved and cared for were there for him. Thinking about them now, he knew they were all dead and that in order to see his beloved Grannie again, he'd have to travel back in time. He wasn't even sure if that was at all possible. His chest ached at the loss. If he couldn't get back, then he'd have to make this his home and he'd fill his life with new people. He'd like those people to be Tessa and John, but he wasn't sure what would happen once things were settled and John didnae need his services any longer. With those thoughts hanging heavy on his mind, Braeden made his way back up the stairs. Briefly stopping in front of Tessa's room, he placed a gentle hand on the door, before returning to his own bed and a restless night's sleep.

CHAPTER *12*

*D*O YE MIND if I join ye, lass?" When Braeden spied Tessa heading back to the McTavish residence, he'd swiftly caught up with her.

Tessa smiled and shook her head. He saw something in the tilt of her head and the gleam in her eyes that caught him off guard. Or was it perhaps simply wishful thinking on his part. She continued walking at a good clip, but he kept up easily, his imaginings outpacing his legs.

His first few days at The Albannach, Braeden thought his head might explode with the constant sounds of people talking all around him. His ears hurt from the ringing, clanging and music of the slot machines and bars. His nose itched from the unfamiliar odors of cigarette smoke mixed with food and perfume. Braeden was a quick study and after just a short time he learned the names of all the new and unusual things he saw, heard and smelled. He wanted to fit in and so, no matter how shocked and amazed he may be feeling inside, on the outside he kept a controlled and measured expression on his face and it was taking a toll on him, whether he wished to admit it or not.

A few more steps and they'd be there. He'd quickly come to think of this haven amidst the clamor as home. The relief he felt when he passed through the doors of the McTavish private quarters was most welcome. He felt like he could breathe again. The ringing in his ears slowly subsided and the rigid position his shoulders had taken melted back to normal.

He could feel Tessa's eyes on him and based on her concerned face, Braeden understood Tessa was worried about him and it touched his heart and soul, so much so he wished to ease her fears with one of his rarely seen smiles.

"Are you okay, Braeden?" Tessa's furrowed brow relaxed somewhat.

"Fine, lass." His light and easy tone was an effort to show her how relaxed he was. As a warrior in his own time he had learned the fine art of only allowing others to see you as strong and unafraid. He opened himself up just a bit for Tessa. He'd be strong for her, protect her and, if she'd let him, he'd love her. He gazed into her eyes and she met his for a split second before quickly averting them to scan the room. It didn't matter that she avoided him now, because he'd noted her sharp intake of breath and the jump of the pulse in her throat. Braeden was a perceptive man. He knew the look of a woman who wanted him, but who fought it. He'd seen it before, but usually on the face of a woman who belonged to another man. Tessa had belonged to Danny, or maybe she never really had, but Danny was gone now in the midst of some very strange happenings. He'd help John solve this puzzle and then, he'd made up his mind, he would make Tessa his. He doubted she would fight it. There was something between them and he wanted to explore it further.

Much to Braeden's surprise, when he sat down, Tessa came up behind him and began massaging his shoulders. "You look so tense and you've been working so hard. Your shoulders are all in knots."

He was speechless. All he could manage to get out of his mouth was, "Mmmm…"

"Take your shirt off. I'll be right back." She hummed happily as she left the room.

Braeden peeled his shirt off and laid it on the arm of the chair. His cock was standing at attention now and he realized he'd better hide the evidence of his desire from Tessa as best he could. He took the shirt and draped it over his lap.

"I'm back. I wanted to get some massage oil. You just sit there and relax." Tessa squirted some oil into the palms of her hands and rubbed them together, warming the oil.

Braeden didn't think relaxing was going to be possible. Her hands on his neck and back were soft and warm, sending signals to his core that he wasn't sure he could fight. He couldn't observe what she was doing, he could only feel it, and he wanted more than anything to see her face as she worked on his sore muscles. Gazing across the room, he spotted a mirror and smiled. Now he could watch her as she ministered to him. Her eyes were closed, her head tipped to the side. A look of pleasure was on her face as her hands slowly and masterfully traced every muscle across his shoulders and back. Tessa slowly slid soft fingers in small circles and then larger circles to his sides. He watched as she slid her tongue across her lips, wetting them in a most sensual manner. Braeden groaned in pleasure.

"Are you okay? I'm not doing this too hard, am I?"

She was so sweet and innocent and had no idea what she was really doing to him. "Nae." It was all he could manage to say.

"I need a massage table. That way you could lie down and I could do this better."

"I dinnae ken how you could do this any better, Tessa."

"You like it!" She sounded surprised at this.

"Aye. Why wouldnae I?" In fact he liked it so much that if she didn't stop soon, he was likely to pull her down into his lap and make love to her right here in the middle of the living room.

TESSA WAS SURPRISED when Braeden asked her to stop. She'd been enjoying the feel of him beneath her fingers. As a matter of fact, she was hoping it would go further than just a massage. She took a deep breath and grabbed the towel she'd thrown over her shoulder to wipe her hands. She wasn't sure, but she'd thought Braeden was getting turned on by her massage. Maybe she was just imagining things because he'd ultimately asked her to stop. Tessa plopped herself down on the floor in front of him and her breath caught in her throat as she saw the look of desire in his eyes. This time she didn't look away, instead she held his gaze and then getting on her knees she placed herself between his legs. She hoped she wasn't reading him incorrectly, but she wasn't going to stop now. Tessa put her arms around his neck and leaning in, she tentatively kissed him on the lips. As she did, she thought, *what if he doesn't want this? What if I'm making a mistake?* She needn't have worried, because in the next breath, Braeden was crushing her to him and passionately returning her kiss. Hands shaking, Tessa ran her fingers through his hair as he held her to him with one large hand placed on her back and the other at her hip. Entangled as they were in each other, they slowly made their way to the floor. Braeden was careful not to crush her, which Tessa could have cared less about.

She wanted to feel every inch of him on top of her. She could feel the wanting between his legs as she could feel it between her own, and excitement ran through her. She wanted him and she didn't care about anything else except having him. Braeden growled as he nibbled on her earlobe and then, pushing her hair aside, slid his tongue down the side of her neck. She shivered in anticipation as he made his way slowly but deliberately down to her chest and opening the buttons of her blouse, he pushed her bra aside and nipped lightly at her dusky pink nipple. Tessa moaned, overcome with desire, causing Braeden's hardened manhood to jump. Any thoughts Tessa may have been having about whether or not this was a good idea were being pushed further and further out of her mind. The aching and tingling between her thighs was seeing to that. Braeden suddenly raised his head as if he was listening to something. Tessa couldn't imagine why he'd stopped and was just about to pull his head back down when she heard it too. The sound of John McTavish singing joyfully as he headed for the front door. Tessa jumped up, leaving Braeden in a heap on the floor. She grabbed the towel and massage oil and ran for the bathroom.

TIMING WAS EVERYTHING as Braeden had come to understand and it was obvious that this had not been the right time to seduce or be seduced by John McTavish's daughter. He quickly threw his shirt back on and waited for John to open the door. "Braeden, there you are. Isn't it a beautiful day?" He glanced around the room. "Where's Tessa?"

"Bathroom," Braeden responded as he tried to calm his breathing and look as if he hadn't just been about to take this man's daughter right here on the floor.

"Tessa!" John called in the direction of the bathroom. "I'll be right out, Da!" Tessa called back.

"Why are ye so happy, John?" Braeden raked his fingers through his hair as he got his breathing under control. He hadn't seen John in such a good mood since he'd arrived. The casino problems, along with Danny's death and the disappearance of one of his cashiers, had been overwhelming for both Tessa and John.

"I've just received good news, Braeden. I wanted to share it with both of you. We'll wait for Tessa and then I'll tell you." He sat down, sniffing the air. "Something smells sweet. You haven't started wearing cologne have you Braeden?"

He hoped he didn't look as guilty as he felt standing there fidgeting with his shirt. He'd been in such a hurry to get it back on that he wasn't sure whether it was backwards and inside out. A few more tugs and pulls told him he needn't worry.

John watched him closely, appearing puzzled by Braeden's behavior. Or perhaps it was Braeden's own imaginings that caused him to think John was on to him. Braeden, in an effort to get himself under control, went to the kitchen where he got himself a glass of water and downed it before returning to the living room. The two men sat gazing at each other while they waited. Braeden's guilty mind had him believing that John knew exactly what had been happening before his arrival. John sat impatiently tapping his fingers on the arm of the chair but stopped abruptly as Tessa entered the room. Braeden could tell that she had adjusted her clothing and taken the time to wait for her face to lose its flushed appearance. He lifted his lips in a small smile meant only for her eyes and she shyly glanced away.

"Da, what are you so excited about?" She walked to her father and sat on the arm of his chair.

"I've received good news today. The hotel's made a huge profit in the short time we've been open and best of all, we are being featured on several travel blogs today."

"Wow!" Tessa bounced up from the chair.

"That's not all. We've also been voted the number one casino/resort in Vegas and the local news is going to do a story on us. With any luck it'll make it to one of the national morning shows. Isn't that wonderful?"

Tessa was beaming now. "I'm so happy for you, Da! That's exciting news." She took her father's hands in hers.

"Be happy for us all, Tessa, not just me. This has been my dream, but it wouldn't be possible without you and all the others who work for us."

"Well, it's not a dream anymore. It's a reality. It's something to be really proud of."

"I've invited travel writers from all over to join us here next weekend. We'll show them the reason why we're number one and they'll help us spread the word to every corner of the earth."

"We should have a meeting to tell all the department heads what's coming up so they'll be prepared to wine and dine these writers."

"I agree. Can I count on you to coordinate that?" John asked.

"Of course. It's about time we had something good happen."

"Braeden, thank you for watching over my Tessa. You've done a great job of taking care of her. I know you'll continue to do so."

"Aye. You can rest assured I will." He snuck a look at Tessa who was looking quite uncomfortable and he felt badly that he'd taken advantage of the situation. He should have maintained his composure and been strong enough to resist the primal urges he felt whenever he was around her. John had entrusted him with his daughter's care and he'd taken advantage of that trust.

"Shall we have dinner together tonight? Champagne to celebrate?" John was obviously delighted at the day's news and he wanted to share it with the two of them.

"Sounds good to me," Tessa said. Braeden nodded in John's direction.

"Good. I'll call the maitre'd at Skarba and tell him to expect us. You both need to go get cleaned up and we'll meet back here in 30 minutes. Does that give you enough time, Tessa?"

"Yes, Da. I'll be ready." Tessa sounded a bit exasperated with her father's obvious teasing.

"Off with you then." John shushed them out of the room with his hands. Braeden followed Tessa up the stairs and when they reached her room, he knew he had to say something. "Tessa, this cannae happen again. Yer father wouldnae approve and I cannae do anything that would be disrespectful of him. I hope ye understand."

Tessa's eyes began to tear and he felt terrible that he was hurting her, but it was for her own good. She got a hold of herself and as she closed the door in his face, he heard her say, "We'll see about that."

He chuckled to himself. She was a feisty one and he had no doubt that she was used to getting what she wanted. While he wanted more than anything to give it to her, he simply couldn't betray John's faith in him.

Chapter *13*

ETECTIVE NANCE PACED back and forth in front of his desk, reminding Tessa of a caged lion. "Miss McTavish, I'm sure you understand that the family and close friends of victims are usually the first people we speak with in regard to their murder."

"Yes, of course." Tessa nodded her understanding.

"You were engaged to Mr. Madden. Is that correct?"

"I was, but I received a text from him telling me that he no longer wished to marry me."

"Did you have an argument?"

"No. It was quite a surprise to me."

"I see. When was the last time you saw Mr. Madden, Tessa?"

"I hadn't seen him since Valentine's Day, after his show."

"Did everything seem alright with him at that time?"

"Yes. We had a very nice evening."

"Was there anyone else with you?"

"My friends Kelly and Braeden were with us."

"So it was a double date?"

"I guess you could call it that."

"Did Mr. Madden say or do anything at all that might lead you to believe there was something wrong?"

"No. That night he was fine. Nothing happened out of the ordinary."

"But other nights he wasn't fine?"

"He had been acting strangely for a few weeks prior to his…" Tessa hesitated. It was still hard to believe someone had murdered Danny. "Death."

"In what way?"

"He was kind of off in his own little world. He was abrupt with me and rude with our friends."

"Can you think of any reason he might have behaved that way?"

"At first I thought it was because of Braeden, but then I realized he had been doing it before Braeden even entered the picture."

"Braeden? The man who double-dated with you?"

"Yes. He works for my father at the resort. He's in charge of security."

"And you're friends with this man and Danny didn't like it."

"I don't think he did, but as I said, he had already been behaving oddly."

"Did the four of you go out together after that?"

"No. We had planned to, but I couldn't get a hold of Danny. He wasn't answering my texts or phone calls."

"It didn't worry you that Mr. Madden wasn't happy to have the company on your dates?"

"No. My father wanted Braeden to tag along with me to make sure I was okay. I didn't want to tell Danny, but my father was concerned for my safety."

"Did your father have a problem with Danny?"

"Well, like any father, he wanted his little girl to be happy and he wanted to be sure Danny was the right man for me. He wasn't sure Danny could protect me if need be."

"Protect you from what, Miss McTavish?"

"I don't really know. I think he was just being extra cautious with the opening of the new resort and everything. He's always been very protective of me."

"Miss McTavish, when Danny sent you the text breaking off your engagement, were you upset with him?"

"I was upset with the way he did it, but not about what he said in his text. I had been planning to break up with him. I wanted to tell him in person, but I couldn't get a hold of him."

"You received the text in the morning you say?"

"Yes, I did."

"Did Danny make you mad enough to kill him, Miss McTavish?"

Tessa was shocked at Detective Nance's directness. She had no idea this interview was going to turn out like this. "No! Absolutely not! I had no reason to kill him. I just told you I was going to break off the engagement myself and I hadn't been able to get in touch with him at all before I read the text."

"Can you prove it?"

"Yes, of course. You can see for yourself on my phone and per my father's directions, I was being followed everywhere by Braeden MacDonald. He can vouch for me."

"I'll need to speak with him."

"He's waiting outside for me." Tessa pointed back towards the door.

Detective Nance went to the door and opened it. He went into the outer office, but Tessa could still hear him.

"Are you Mr. MacDonald?" he asked.

"Aye. I am." Braeden answered.

"Please join us in my office." Detective Nance stood in the doorway with his arm extended, showing Braeden in.

As Tessa waited for Braeden to come in, she worried that he might say something about time traveling that would make Detective Nance think he was crazy. She hadn't done anything that should cause her to be a suspect, but she understood that Detective Nance wouldn't be doing his job if he didn't look under every rock for answers to this mystery.

Braeden passed Detective Nance as he entered. He gazed at Tessa with a questioning look, which turned to one of concern when he saw her furrowed brow.

"Mr. MacDonald, please have a seat. I'm Detective Nance." He held his hand out to Braeden, who grasped it in a strong handshake. The two men sized each other up over that handshake. "Miss McTavish was just telling me that you have been going everywhere with her at her father's request. Is that true?"

"Aye. Mr. McTavish hired me as hotel security and one of my jobs is to be certain that Tessa is safe."

"Do you know why he is concerned for her safety?"

"Because she's his daughter." Braeden's terse response did not endear him to the detective.

"I'm serious, Mr. MacDonald."

"I ken ye are and so am I. Are ye a father, detective?"

"I am. I have two boys and a girl." He proudly showed them the photos on the wall behind his desk.

"And would ye nae do anything to make sure yer children were safe in this world?"

"I would. Point taken. On the night that Mr. Madden was murdered, where were you and Miss McTavish?"

"We were at The Albannach. We finished our jobs for the day and we went back to the McTavish apartments to have dinner. We watched a movie and then I escorted Miss McTavish up to bed."

"What time was that?"

"Around midnight."

"And you're sure she didn't sneak out in the middle of the night?"

"Positive. I'm a light sleeper and I hear everything. I would have known immediately if she was *sneaking out* as you put it."

"Miss McTavish, did Danny have any enemies that you were aware of?"

"No. Most people liked him. He was a celebrity and people were always trying to be near him. They loved him. Of course, there are always a few kooks on the internet, but they never did anything more than post negative comments about his show or his physical appearance."

"That's all the questions I have for you at the moment, Miss McTavish, Mr. MacDonald. Please stay in the Las Vegas area in case I need to speak with you again."

Tessa and Braeden rose to go. Braeden placed a calming hand at the small of her back and guided her through the doors and out of the police station.

"That was weird," Tessa said, shaking her head in disbelief.

"Do they think you killed Danny?"

"I don't know. I don't think they have a clue who did it and they're talking to everyone who knew him. The fact that he broke off our engagement just prior to his murder shines a light on me, even though I didn't get the text until later."

"Let's go back to The Albannach. Your father must be worried about you."

"I'm sure he is. He won't like hearing that I'm a suspect."

BRAEDEN DIDN'T UNDERSTAND why the police would think that someone as sweet and kind as Tessa would have anything at all to do with Danny's murder. He'd do whatever was necessary to prove that she was innocent.

They entered The Albannach through the employee entrance and headed straight for John's office. Braeden kept a vigilant watch on everything, making sure that nothing was amiss as they entered the private area of the hotel, which was off limits to hotel guests.

Kelly smiled brightly at the two of them as they opened the door to John's outer offices. "Good morning, you two." Neither Braeden nor Tessa returned her smile. "Or is it?"

"Is my Da in his office?" Tessa appeared worried and it tore at Braeden's heart.

"He is. Go on in." Kelly gave Braeden a quizzical look. He didn't like leaving her with questions, but they had to see John. He'd speak with her later.

"Tessa. Braeden. I've been looking all over for you two. Is everything alright?"

"We've been at the police station, Da." Tessa wearily sank into one of the leather arm chairs in front of her father's desk. Braeden took the other one. "The police station? Did they get Danny's killer?"

"No. They didn't and worse yet, I think I'm a suspect."

"What? How could you possibly be a suspect?"

"They think that because he broke off our engagement that I would have been angry enough to kill him." Tessa leaned forward and put her head in her hands.

Braeden understood her weariness and he laid a protective hand on her back. "I'm not from yer time, so I dinnae ken what we can do to help."

"We may need to do some investigating of our own." John glanced lovingly at his daughter. "Not you, Tessa. Braeden and I will try to figure out who might have killed Danny and why. Don't worry; they couldn't possibly arrest you. They don't have any evidence pointing to you as the killer. They're just grasping at straws."

Tessa lifted her head. "I know they are, but it still bothers me that they think I could do something like that."

"They're just doing their jobs, my love. There have been some strange goings on around here and we're going to get to the bottom of it. You should take the rest of the day off. You could use the rest."

"Thanks, Da. I appreciate the offer, but I can't sit around doing nothing. It's better for me to work. Besides, there are lots of things that need to be done. Did we ever figure out how the safe was being manipulated?"

"No, but I'm starting to think it may have had something to do with Danny's murder. Have you been able to speak with Kenneth yet?"

"He wasn't home when we went there yesterday, but he should be at work this today. Braeden and I will go see if we can find him."

"Let me know what he has to say. Braeden keep a close watch on my little girl. She needs you now more than ever."

"Aye. She'll never leave my sight."

AT THE CASHIER'S office, Tessa and Braeden passed through the ornate doors and into a very busy room. Margaret was moving from cashier to cashier. She handed them each a piece of paper and then waited patiently while they counted the cash in their drawers and compared it with the printout for their station. As she came to the last cashier, she looked up and, seeing Tessa, said something to the cashier and headed their way.

"Good morning." She nodded to both Tessa and Braeden.

"Good morning, Margaret? How's everything going so far?"

"So far so good. I was just checking the receipts from each of the cashiers. Everything seems to be in order."

"Anymore funny stuff with the safe?"

"No. Not today."

"We were wondering if we could speak with Kenneth."

"He's not here. He was on the schedule for today, but he never came in. I called his wife and she said she hadn't seen him. Said he didn't come home last night."

Tessa exchanged a concerned glance with Braeden. "Has he ever done this before?"

"No. He was one of my more reliable cashiers. Although, we've only been open a short while. I don't know what he was like at his last job."

Tessa could see the wheels turning in Braeden's head. "I don't like this," he said.

"Neither do I. Margaret, if he comes in, please let us know right away."

"Of course." She went back to the last cashier and they began going over the receipts.

"Should we go back to his house to speak with his wife?"

"I don't know what good that would do." Braeden escorted Tessa out of the cashier's office.

"I don't either, but I could call her on the phone. I'll get her number from human resources and give her a call. You know, tell her to get in touch with us if she hears from him."

"Human resources?" Braeden was obviously still baffled by some of the language he heard used around the resort.

"Human resources. Personnel. It's the department responsible for keeping track of our employees. We went there to get his address. They'll have his home phone number and perhaps even his cell phone number."

"Lead the way." Braeden extended his arm signaling for Tessa to go ahead of him. They headed back to the employees only entrance of the resort offices and straight through to the Human Resources department. This was probably the largest department at the casino. There were dozens of people working at desks that were separated into cubicles throughout the large open room. Tessa noted that Braeden, in his usual *nothing surprises me* way, gazed calmly around as if he'd seen it all a million times before. She smiled at him, knowing that it was probably a reflex that he had practiced back in his own time—never appear surprised at anything.

She asked the first girl they came to if she could get Kenneth's phone numbers and contact info and it was handed to her without question. Everyone knew who Tessa was as she'd taken the time to personally meet every one of them before the casino opened for business.

"Thanks. How's everything going? Are you happy here with us?" Tessa asked.

"Yes. Very happy. Love my job." The girl beamed at Tessa and she could see there was no doubt this particular young lady was telling the truth.

"Good. We're happy to have you here." Tessa smiled warmly at the girl and then, turning to Braeden, she signaled him that it was time to leave. Once out in the hallway, she felt comfortable talking about it. "We've got both phone numbers. Let's go back to my office and we'll try to call him. I don't have a good feeling about this."

Braeden nodded his agreement and followed Tessa as they made their way to her office, which was located in the same wing as her father's. Tessa spent very little time there and she didn't have an assistant like her father had. If she needed help with anything, Kelly was always willing to lend a hand. Entering her office, she motioned for Braeden to close the door as she went around her desk and sat down. Braeden took the chair on the opposite side of her desk.

"I'll try his cell phone first." She dialed and waited only a moment. "It goes straight to voice mail. "I'll try his home number." Again, she waited, but this time someone answered. "Hello, is Kenneth there? This is Tessa McTavish. He didn't come to work today and we were wondering if he was ill."

"Can you hang on a minute?" The person on the other end of the phone called to someone else.

"Hello? This is Mrs. Carra. Can I help you?"

"This is Tessa McTavish. We were by yesterday afternoon to see your husband."

"Yes. I remember." Her voice trembled and before long she was sobbing into the phone.

"Is everything alright? You sound upset." This was concerning.

"I am. I guess you haven't heard yet. My husband is dead. They don't know what happened, but they found his body thrown in a dumpster behind The Albannach."

"What?" Tessa couldn't believe her ears. Why hadn't anyone notified her father? "I'm so sorry, Mrs. Carra. If there's anything we can do to help, please let us know." She hung up with a look of horror on her face.

Braeden, who had been listening, shot up from his chair to go to her. "Is something wrong?" He placed a warm hand on her shoulder and it calmed her almost instantly.

"Yes. Kenneth is dead. Someone murdered him and dumped his

body behind the casino in a dumpster. I can't believe no one notified us." She rose and headed for the door.

"Where are we going?" Braeden followed along behind.

"To the dumpster. I want to know what's going on. The police might still be there. It's an active crime scene I'm assuming."

CHAPTER *14*

𝒰NFAMILIAR WITH SOME of the things he was hearing, Braeden kept his mouth shut and let Tessa lead the way. She obviously had a mission and although he wasn't sure what it was she wished to accomplish, he would be there for her if she needed him.

As they rounded the corner of the back parking lot, the dumpsters were in sight as were an army of police officers. They had the area cordoned off and as Tessa stormed up to them, Detective Nance broke away from the others to greet her.

"What's going on here and why haven't we been notified? I just found out from Mr. Carra's wife that he was found dead here in one of the dumpsters. Is that correct?"

"I'm afraid so." Detective Nance distractedly glanced back at the crime scene.

"Well, what happened? And why weren't we notified right away?" It was obvious that Tessa was becoming impatient with Detective Nance.

"We don't really know and I have more important things to do right now than running in to tell you what happened. I'd have gotten around to it as soon as we wrapped things up here. The coroner's office is on the way to collect the body and in the meantime, we're searching for any clues we can find."

From the looks of it, they hadn't been very successful. Tessa was able to get a good look at Kenneth's body, which hadn't yet been moved from the dumpster, and there didn't seem to be any wounds visible on his body. To her untrained eye, he looked like he was merely sleeping. If he had died of natural causes, there's no way he would have climbed into the dumpster to die. Something was up. First Danny, now Kenneth. He was the only one other than Margaret who had seen the tumblers on the safe moving on their own. Could his death be related to that incident? She certainly thought *both* deaths could be related to it, along with the missing man from The King Arthur.

"Detective, we had a strange incident occur at the casino the other day. The tumblers on the safe were being remotely tampered with. The only two people to see it were Margaret Camden, our manager and Mr. Carra. We went to his home to speak with him about it, but he wasn't there. When he didn't show up for work this morning, we were worried. I wonder if his death had something to do with what he saw."

"How could someone remotely mess with your safe? That seems absurd."

"You would think so, but two people saw it happening."

"Okay. Then I guess the better question would be why? Why would someone mess with the tumblers from another location. Even if they opened the safe they'd be too far away to do anything about it."

"Agreed. Unless they have someone here at The Albannach to help them."

"We'll look into it, Miss McTavish. We'll want to talk to you more about this whole thing and we should probably speak with Margaret Camden."

"Fine. I'll be right here at the resort." She handed him her business card for a second time. "In case you don't have my numbers with you, that's my cell phone number. I have my phone with me at all times."

"Thanks. Now if you'll excuse me, I'd like to finish up here."

Tessa and Braeden turned away and headed back inside. "I find it so strange that all of this is happening. Who could possibly be behind it?"

"I believe your father thinks it could be Niall Campbell. Maybe we should pay him a visit."

"I think you're right."

SAM STOPPED THE limo in front of The Las Vegas Society for Magick and Sorcery. It was a large pinkish, stucco building with stark white columns and ornate decorative features around the doors and windows. They climbed the steps to the oversized, brass double doors, which automatically opened as they reached them. Braeden was on the alert, eyeing the entryway with suspicion. They were in enemy territory. As far as he was concerned, no Campbell was to be trusted.

The foyer was grand with marble floors in shades of beige, brown and black on white. Two curving stairways led up to a second-floor balcony that overlooked the entry, and standing front and center was Niall Campbell.

"What a lovely surprise. To what do I owe this honor, Tessa?" Niall began to descend the stairway while Braeden, along with Tessa, waited below.

"Hello, Niall," Tessa said. Braeden could feel her tension rising the closer he got.

"My dear, I wish ye'd called to let me know ye were coming. I would have had my chef prepare us a lovely luncheon."

"It was just a spur of the moment decision. I was wondering if we could talk to you about something?" Tessa was doing her best to act as if nothing was wrong.

Niall turned to Braeden. "Ye must be Braeden MacDonald. I'm very please to finally meet ye." He extended his hand to Braeden, who wondered how Niall knew who he was. They hadn't been introduced and there was no reason he should have known about him. After a brief hesitation, he grasped Niall's hand in his own. "That's quite the grip ye've got there." Niall winced in pain and quickly extricated his hand.

"Where are ye from, Braeden?"

"Scotland." His answer was short and to the point.

"Yes. I know that. Where in Scotland?"

"Glencoe." Again, Braeden kept his answers short. What he really wanted to do was to wrap his fingers around Niall Campbell's throat, but he knew that would not be acceptable in this time.

"Site of the famous massacre. I hope that the fact I'm a Campbell won't get in the way of us being friends."

Tessa jumped in at that point. "Of course not, that's old news, isn't that right, Braeden." She raised an eyebrow in his direction and he understood her message clearly.

"Aye. Old news." An undercurrent of rage ran through Braeden, but he controlled it.

Niall let loose with an uncomfortable laugh. The tension filling the air seemed ready to explode. "Well, then…"

Braeden's slow smile didn't reach his eyes, and was meant to cause Niall more discomfort than he was already feeling. It seemed to be working.

"Come. This way. We'll sit in the drawing room."

Tessa glanced at Braeden and rolled her eyes. The first time he'd seen her do it, he hadn't known quite what to think, but he was learning and he quietly chuckled at her antics.

"Niall, there have been some unusual things happening lately that seem to be centered on me and The Albannach. I was wondering if you'd heard anything about it from any of the other members of your group."

"No." Niall adjusted the cuffs of his shirt as he spoke. "What unusual things are ye speaking of?"

"Well, Danny's murder for one thing."

"Yes. That was quite unfortunate. It's been all over the news." Niall glanced from Tessa to Braeden and back again. When neither one spoke, he continued. "You said *things*. I'm assuming there's more than just Danny's death on yer mind."

Tessa cleared her throat. "We've also had something happen with our safe." She paused for a moment, eyeing Niall in the process. "Someone was spinning the dials remotely. Two people saw it and now one of them is dead. His death was also suspicious."

"That is strange. Who do ye think is behind it?"

"I don't know. That's why we're here. I was wondering if anyone at The Society of Magick and Sorcery may have been acting strangely lately. Or possibly may have said something that, thinking back on it, you might find suspicious."

Braeden watched Niall and was impressed with his ability to act as if he had absolutely no idea what was going on. Braeden was fairly sure he did.

Niall gazed up at the ceiling as if he were trying to recall something that might be helpful. Eventually he lowered his eyes. "I'm afraid I can't think of anything at all that would be useful to ye. Perhaps the police can be of more help than I can."

"They're working on it. We just thought we'd help out by asking around."

"I wish I could be more helpful, but I really don't know anything. I'll keep my ears open though and if anything comes up, I'll give ye a call. Would either of ye care to join me for a cocktail?" Niall walked to the bar by the window, waving his hand before it. The doors to the lower cabinet opened, revealing crystal glasses and decanters filled with alcohol.

Tessa was just about to say no, but Braeden jumped in before she could open her mouth. "Whiskey," he said.

"My favorite," Niall responded. "Tessa? Wine or something else perhaps?"

"Wine would be lovely, Niall."

He went to the bar and poured the drinks. Handing them to Tessa and Braeden, he then went back for his own. "Ye know, I'm wondering about something." He took a sip of his whiskey and then very pointedly gazed at Braeden, before turning his attention to Tessa. "Do either of ye believe in time travel?" The casual way in which he asked was obviously meant to solicit a response from them. Neither one moved.

Braeden sipped his drink and leveled a deadly glare in Niall's direction. "Just curious, ye know. We once had a member who claimed to be a time traveler. He said he was from Scotland. The late seventeenth century. He was also a Campbell. He had a most unusual watch that he said could transport him through time. Isn't that just the most incredible thing ye've ever heard?"

Tessa's glass had hardly left her lips while Niall was speaking. She coughed in response.

"I'm sorry. Are ye alright, Tessa? Let me get you a napkin." Niall retrieved a napkin from the bar and handed it to her.

She accepted it and it and used it to dab at her lips. Braeden could see her stealing a look in his direction. "Why do ye tell us this?"

"Well, because now that I've had a moment to think about odd goings on, he came to mind."

Tessa and Braeden sat silently waiting for him to continue. Niall seemed happy to keep them waiting. As a matter of fact, he behaved as if he weren't going to continue at all.

"Go on, please." Tessa broke the silence. "This is quite interesting, isn't it Braeden?"

"Aye. 'Tis."

"I'm sorry. My mind drifted off to tonight's meeting. All of our members will be joining me. Ye're welcome to stay if ye like."

"Continue on with yer time travel tale." Braeden's patience was wearing thin and it showed.

"As I was saying, he had a watch that helped him time travel. I didn't believe him, but oddly enough he disappeared one day, never to be seen or heard from again."

"Did ye see him disappear?" Braeden questioned.

"No. He never came around again and we couldn't find him despite our best efforts. If he did actually time travel, he told me that the watch was only set to allow the bearer passage to another time once every twelve years. Ye see the dial, which was much like any other watch, moved differently. The hour hands were actually representative of the passage of one year. So the hands of the watch had to go all the way around the dial before it could be used again. Fascinating, isn't it?"

"Hmmm…" Tessa put her glass down on the ornate little end table next to her chair. "Did you call the police about this missing man?"

"No. For all I know he could have decided Las Vegas wasn't for him and headed off to a more suitable destination."

"What did it look like? The watch." Braeden was curious if it was the same one he'd received from his Grannie.

"Let me see if I can recall. It was quite beautiful. I do remember that much. It was covered in beautiful jewels. I believe a bird was depicted on the outer casing. I only ever saw it from a distance. He wouldn't allow anyone to touch it and he never opened it. He said if he did, it could stop time." Niall chuckled at that. "Can ye imagine being able to stop time. Oh, the things ye could accomplish if only it were possible." He glanced Braeden's way. "Ye don't happen to have a watch, do ye?"

"What business is it of yers?" Braeden stood and Niall shrank back, a brief moment of fright on his face.

"I was just wondering. I didn't mean to upset ye."

"Tessa, 'tis time to go." Braeden snarled.

She placed her glass on the table and without question, she began heading for the door. "Thank you for the wine, Niall. I believe we need to be on our way."

Braeden grabbed her elbow and practically lifted her off the ground as he hurried her out the door. Niall stood silently by until they reached the door. "Please come back and visit any time. My doors are always open to ye. To both of ye."

"WHAT WAS THAT all about?" Tessa asked as she unsuccessfully tried to extricate herself from Braeden's grip. "You're hurting me," she winced.

"My apologies." Braeden released her arm. "That man knows exactly how to get under me skin. I tried me best to nae let him, but I'd had enough."

"He knows something, Braeden. Especially with all that talk about a watch. Your watch is the watch he was talking about, isn't it?"

"Aye. And I believe he wants it."

"No doubt he does. Especially if it can do what he thinks it can. We have to make sure he never gets his hands on it." Braeden held the door open for her to enter the limo and then climbed in beside her. "Who do you think the man is that he was speaking of?"

"I believe it was me father. He left the watch to me, but me father was nae a Campbell. I dinnae ken what he meant by that." Tessa could see that Braeden was upset.

"It's okay. We'll get to the bottom of this."

"Yer father must know of this. Why would he keep this from me?"

"I don't know, but we're going to find out." Tessa put a comforting hand on his arm and was immediately affected by the strength she felt there. It was one thing to see those muscles and admire them, but to actually feel them. Wow! They were rock hard, but the skin covering them was silky soft to the touch. Her mind wandered because her hands couldn't. She closed her eyes and imagined herself safely co-cooned in his strong embrace. Braeden's hand covered hers, leaving her heart pounding in her chest and making it difficult to breath. *Relax,* she told herself. She slowly took a deep breath and turned her focus toward finding out what Niall had been talking about. If she were Braeden, she didn't think she'd be sitting there quite as calmly, but he was full of surprises. He had been since day one. Beneath that calm exterior there was a volcano about to erupt, but he'd never show it. That would be giving away his power and she knew him well enough to know that was not going to happen.

THE MOMENT SHE saw Tessa and Braeden leaving the mansion, Margaret Camden slid below window-level in her car seat. She had to see Niall, but she absolutely had to remain hidden from view until they departed. If they saw her there, it would surely pique their curiosity about her relationship with Niall and that wouldn't be a good thing for either one of them.

After they drove away she waited a few extra minutes to be sure they wouldn't see her and, exiting her vehicle, she hurried to the entry-way. Niall was waiting for her as she opened the door.

"Niall." Margaret ran into his arms. "Is everything okay. I saw Tessa leaving." Niall lifted her chin and gazed lovingly into her eyes. "Margaret, my love, there is nae need to worry. They're merely testing the waters to see if they can catch me and believe me when I tell ye, they willnae. My sorcery will win out in the end. Ye'll see."

Margaret knew he was right, but still, some of the things that were happening hadn't been in the original plan. For one thing, no one was supposed to die. "Why did Danny and Kenneth have to die? I thought we had agreed that it wasn't necessary. And what about Mr. Winchester? I haven't seen him at the casino for a few days."

"Winchester willnae be back. Once I found out he was working for McTavish he had to go."

"Is he dead too?" Margaret began to shake in Niall's arms.

"I'm afraid so. It couldn't be helped. You and I are the most im-portant element of my plan, Margaret. You understand, don't ye?" His soft, controlled voice calmed her.

"I do, Niall. I'm just afraid we'll be caught." Tears spilled from

Margaret's eyes as she spoke.

Niall produced a hankie out of thin air. "Here, my love. Dinnae weep. All will be well, ye'll see."

Margaret believed in Niall and trusted him, but she never expected that he would kill people to get what he wanted. "I feel so badly about Kenneth. He had a wife and children."

"You are a sweet woman with a soft heart, Margaret, it's one of your most endearing qualities, but this had to be done. Kenneth made the unfortunate mistake of seeing the tumblers move, forcing you to report it to McTavish. If they had questioned him about it, suspicion may have landed on ye, my sweet. I couldnae have that. I love ye, Margaret and I cannae be parted from ye. So, ye see, 'tis important ye remain a trusted employee. As for Madden, he planned to betray me. All I asked of him was to marry Tessa. Ye wouldn't think that was such a difficult task, but then he failed to tell me, or anyone it would seem, that he was already married. Tessa was my key to John McTavish. I couldn't take the chance that he would tell her about our plans, so I used my magic to send him to his rest. I then, of course, tried to put the suspicion on Tessa by sending her a text message from him, breaking off their engagement."

"I know the police questioned her, but I haven't heard anything else about it. As a matter of fact, when the police were at The Albannach investigating Kenneth's death, I'm pretty sure she told them about the tumblers." Margaret began to tremble again. "What if they find out I'm involved, Niall. What if they arrest me?"

"Dinnae fear, Margaret. They have no evidence. We were merely experimenting with the tumblers to see what we could achieve, but we willnae need to open the vault by such means any longer."

Margaret appeared puzzled by this. "What do you mean? How will you get the money?"

"If I can get my hands on the watch, we won't have to. What luck that it's back here in Las Vegas." Niall smiled triumphantly. "All will be well, my dearest Margaret. We'll use the watch to get all the money we could ever want, and then we'll travel to the future. Just ye and me. Ye'll have everything yer heart could ever desire."

"I'm confused, Niall. What watch is this that you're talking about?"

"Ye werenae part of my life back then, although I wish with all my heart that ye had been." Niall chucked her under the chin and then wrapping an arm around her, led her into his study. "Ye see, a distant ancestor of mine travelled here from the past. He used a watch that I'd heard rumors about throughout my life. I wasn't sure it actually existed, but the family history says that it disappeared in about 1692. The time of the Glencoe Massacre. No one knew what had happened to it, but the legend of the watch was passed down from generation to generation. I had dreamed that someday it would find its way to me and it had with the appearance of Ian Campbell, but he wouldnae part with it. Now I've another chance and I willnae fail this time." He led her to the settee and sat beside her, folding her into his embrace. "Now Margaret, tell me, where would you like to live when this is over? We can go anywhere ye like. What's yer heart's desire?"

CHAPTER 15

The limo let Tessa and Braeden off at the usual entrance and they hurried to John's office. They breezed past Kelly, who seemed confused when they didn't return her cheery greeting. Flinging open John's office doors they surprised him, causing his head to jolt up to see who was arriving.

"Tessa. Braeden. Is something wrong? I heard about Kenneth. Have you any news?" John seemed sincerely distressed at the loss of his employee.

Without fanfare, Tessa simply went for it. "Da, we need to know about Braeden's father."

John rose, coming around to lean back on the front of his desk. "Sit, please." Braeden and Tessa did as he asked and then waited for him to speak. He took his time, obviously weighing what he would tell them.

Unable to wait for him to speak, Braeden asked, "Is it true? Was he a Campbell?"

"I'm sorry Braeden. I didn't say anything earlier because I didn't wish to distress you, knowing how you feel about the Campbells, but in answer to your question, yes. He was."

The veins in Braeden's forearms bulged as he fisted his hands. Tessa laid her hands over his. "Calm down, Braeden. Let Da tell you what he knows."

"He was a Campbell, but don't hold that against him, lad. He loved your mother very much, so much so that he betrayed his clan name to be with her. You were the result of that union."

Braeden sank back into the chair. The expression on his face was unreadable. "My father's clan destroyed the MacDonalds. I cannae forgive or forget that. They would have killed me as well, if I hadn't had the watch."

"I know, Braeden. This must be a difficult pill to swallow, but you must know that your father loved you. That's why he gave your Grannie the watch. It was for you all along and he knew that it would save you when you needed it most. He timed his travel precisely; it was important for him to go back when he did since the watch only works every twelve years. He knew the date of the Glencoe Massacre, and he knew he needed to get the watch back at least twelve years before that date, or you would possibly perish at the hands of the Campbells."

"If I didnae have the watch, I wouldnae be here now. The Campbells were upon me and if it werenae for the watch, I would have been shot dead. There was nae other way to escape them." Braeden hung his head, memories of that fateful day bombarding him. Oh, how he wished it could have ended differently, for all of them.

"Da, Niall Campbell knows about the watch. We went to see him today and he denied knowing anything at all about Danny, Kenneth or the safe."

"Tessa, that was a dangerous move on your part. Of course he'd deny knowledge of what's happened and now he knows we're suspicious of him." John raked his hands through his hair, worry etching his face.

"I'm sorry, Da. I guess I was so angry I didn't stop to think of the repercussions of going to see him, but he did mention Braeden's father and the watch. He asked if we believed in time travel and he asked Braeden if he had a watch."

"What did you say?" John seemed to hold his breath waiting for Braeden to answer.

"Nothing. I told him nothing," Braeden answered.

"He knows, Da. That's why he was asking him."

"That is a problem. If he knows you have it, he's likely to try to spirit it away."

"Should we hide it?" Tessa asked.

"That wouldn't do any good. He's a sorcerer. He'd find it in no time."

"If only there was a way to cloak it and keep it safe." Tessa glanced back and forth between the two men.

Braeden, Tessa and John sat in silence. The gravity of the situation weighed heavily on them.

"Do ye ken a sorcerer who would be willing to help? One who wouldnae try to steal the watch from us?" Braeden asked.

John tapped his fingers on the desk. "I just might. I'll contact him. In the meantime, keep a close eye on that watch. We have to keep it away from Niall."

Braeden and Tessa bid goodbye to John, leaving him to work on their problem.

꙰

"DO YOU KNOW the story behind that watch?" Tessa asked.

"Nae. I only know that my Grandmother gave it to me when she knew me to be in danger. She told me to think of me Ma and wish on it. Wish for it to take me to the meadows."

"So that's why you asked about the meadows when you first arrived. You must have been so very confused by it all."

"Aye. I thought I was dead. That I'd gone to hell. Then I saw you and thought I must be in heaven." The twinkle in his eye told Tessa he was having fun with her.

Tessa playfully shoved Braeden and then laughed and shook her head when it didn't move him even a fraction of an inch. "It all makes sense now. You really thought I was an angel. You weren't flirting with me like I thought."

"I did. Now I know the truth. You are an angel. An angel here on earth." Tessa quickly glanced away from Braeden's smoldering eyes. Once again, her pulse quickened and she was finding it hard to breathe. "Braeden, you've got to stop doing this to me."

"What am I doing?" He asked with a lopsided grin on his handsome face.

"You know exactly what you're doing. Don't act all innocent with me."

"I'm anything but innocent, lass. And if it were possible, I'd do a lot more than ruffle yer feathers with me words."

Goosebumps broke out all over Tessa as she imagined just what it might be like to spend a sultry afternoon in bed, making love to Braeden MacDonald. Tessa took a quick peak at Braeden's face just as his finger traced a line up her arm, across her shoulder and under her chin. He lifted her chin so he could look into her eyes. She thought he might kiss her, but then he seemed to think better of it and, as he removed his finger, Tessa sighed her disappointment.

It took a moment for her to gather herself, but once she did Tessa thought about their problem and then had an idea. "You know, I think there's someone we should pay a visit to. He's a magician here at a casino off The Strip. He's not the young, sexy guy who attracts a huge crowd, but he's very good. I think he might be able to help us cloak that watch of yours."

"What if he's working with Niall Campbell?"

"I don't think that's even remotely possible. Niall hates him. They've had a few run-ins over the years. Bobby used to be a member of the Society, but after having a huge argument with Niall, he either walked away or was asked to resign his position. I'm not sure which it was, but there's no love lost between those two."

"Then he sounds like the man to help us." Braeden extended his arm signaling Tessa to lead the way.

She grabbed his hand and secretly smiled to herself when he didn't pull it away. "Let's go then."

THEY ARRIVED AT the Longbow Casino where Bobby Noonan was the headlining magician. He didn't seem at all surprised to see them. He wasn't terribly tall for a man—probably only about five feet six or seven. He had curly, greying hair and blue eyes alive with mischief.

"Tessa! To what do I owe the honor?" Bobby leaned in and kissed Tessa on the cheek. "And who's this mammoth creature you've brought with you?" He sized up Braeden, making a show of craning his neck to see all the way to the top of Braeden's head.

"Hi, Bobby. It's so good to see you." She squeezed his hand in hers. "This is Braeden MacDonald. He's my bodyguard. Dad seems to think I need one."

"Well, he picked a good one, and I believe your father is right. It's wise to keep you safe." Turning his attention on Braeden, he held out his hand to shake and Braeden reciprocated. "I'm pleased to meet you, lad. So, you're a MacDonald are you?"

"Aye. 'Tis good to meet ye, sir."

"I know you didn't come here just to say hello. I was just about to return a call to your father. I imagine you're here on his behalf. Is there some way I can be of service?"

"As a matter of fact, there is." Tessa took a deep breath before relaying Braeden's story and their concern about Niall Campbell. She also told him about Danny and Kenneth, and their mysterious deaths. When she was finished, she glanced at Braeden, who nodded, letting her know she had done a good job.

"So, Niall is up to his old tricks, is he? I can't say I'm surprised. I'm happy you thought to come to me. Most people look on me as a has-been with little or no talent. The Society did an excellent job of slandering me when I left them. I couldn't stay one more minute with that pompous, self-important excuse for a sorcerer."

Bobby's dressing room at the Longbow was tiny and with three people in it, one of them being a six foot four Highlander, it felt a lot like a closet.

"So you'll help us?" Tessa asked hopefully.

"Of course." Bobby squeezed past Braeden to reach a bottle of whiskey he kept on his dressing table. He pulled out three paper cups and filling them, handed one to Tessa and one to Braeden. "To successfully overcoming Niall Campbell and whatever it is he's up to."

The three touched cups and drank. The men finished theirs and Tessa, who'd taken only a tiny sip, screwed up her face and shivered. "I don't know why you all like this stuff so much. It must be an acquired taste." Braeden and Bobby chuckled as she searched the tiny space for a place where she could deposit her still full cup. Braeden came to her rescue, taking it from her and finishing it in one swallow. Tessa looked up at him in astonishment, shaking her head. "Yuck!"

"Shall we find a place that's a bit more roomy to continue our discussion?" Bobby pointed towards the door and then put a hand on Tessa and Braeden to guide them out of the room.

A wave of relief washed over Tessa as they exited the minuscule dressing room. She'd never considered herself claustrophobic before, but she was rethinking it after being in such cramped quarters. "Bobby, you should really talk to my Da about coming to work at The Albannach. I know he'd love to have you."

"I don't know. I'm sort of on the magician black list here in Vegas. I'm afraid if he did hire me, Niall would ruin him."

"I think he already has that in his plans. Do you think he may have been behind the incident with the safe?"

"I'd bet money on it." Bobby chuckled at his own Las Vegas joke.

As they walked, Tessa smiled warmly in his direction. "We should get back to The Albannach and tell Da you're willing to help. Why don't you join us?"

"I've got my show tonight. I'll stop by after that, but before you go, let me cloak that watch of yours." He muttered an incantation that was barely audible before handing the watch back to Braeden. "You'll be able to hide it in plain sight now if you like. Niall and the others at The Society will no longer be able to detect its presence." Bobby lifted Tessa's hand and kissed her knuckles and then bowing reverently, he turned and left them.

"What did you think?" Tessa asked Braeden as they headed back to their limo.

"I believe he's just the man we need to help us."

Braeden placed his hand on the small of her back, a move that always took Tessa's breath away. The warmth of his hand combined with the gentlemanly way he protected her from the casino crowds had her lady parts heating up just in time for their ride back to The Albannach. She was going to have to talk to her father about telling Braeden it was okay for him to pursue her. She couldn't imagine any reason he'd have a problem with it. Braeden's sense of loyalty was honorable, but in this case, she thought it was unnecessary.

In the limo, she took advantage of the opportunity presented by a sharp turn from the driver to lean into Braeden, who placed a protective arm around her. She was going to break him down yet. She let her hand slowly traverse his strong abs and come to rest on the waist of his kilt, noticing some movement from just below. She smiled to herself, knowing she was having as much of an affect on him as he had on her. She made no attempt to move back to her original position. He was simply going to have to deal with her being as close as she was. She was enjoying it way too much to move. They continued on the short drive back to The Albannach with Tessa thoroughly enjoying herself and Braeden seemingly as ill at ease as he could possibly be. Here he was a big strong man and Tessa had him right where she wanted him, wrapped around her little finger.

THE LIMO STOPPED and Braeden peeled Tessa's hand away disconnecting himself as best he could from her grip. Exiting the limo, he took a moment to get his body back under control before reaching a hand inside to help Tessa out and onto the walkway. She smiled sweetly up at him and he silently cursed his rising manhood as it threatened to make another appearance.

Entering the casino through the employee entrance, they headed straight for John's office. As they approached Kelly's desk, she took note of the two of them and then when Tessa wasn't looking, winked at Braeden, who merely rolled his eyes, a move he'd learned from Tessa, and shook his head.

"John's not here right now." Kelly said as Tessa reached for the door handle to his office.

"Where is he?" she asked with a pout on her face.

"He said he had some errands to run and he'd be back within the hour. He only just left, so you'll have a bit of a wait." Kelly appeared ready to burst into laughter at the two of them, but Braeden noted she kept it under control, only showing him that she thought his predicament funny. Their friendship had become more and more comfortable since his arrival and she was very aware of the fact that he was attracted to Tessa. She also knew that he felt he could do nothing about it until they'd taken care of whatever it was that was happening to put her, John and the casino in danger.

"Let's wait for him in my office. Kelly would you call me when he gets back." Tessa headed for the hallway leading to her office.

"Okay. No problem." Kelly called. "Braeden, can I talk to you before you go."

"Aye." He glanced at Tessa's receding backside as she disappeared down the hallway.

"Tessa. I'll be right there."

He waited, but she didn't answer him and he turned back to Kelly with eyebrows raised in question.

"Don't worry. She'll be fine. She's just down the hall," Kelly reassured him.

"I ken she is, but there are some verra powerful men here in Las Vegas who could harm her." Braeden glanced down the hall again.

"What's going on?" Kelly leaned forward, eyes agleam. Braeden had learned that one thing Kelly loved above all else, was what she called gossip.

"I cannae tell ye, Kelly. If I did it may put ye in danger as well, and I wouldnae ever forgive meself if anything happened to ye. Yer man Sean wouldnae either."

"Is it something to do with Niall Campbell? Did he kill Danny and Kenneth?"

"Yer like a dog with a bone, lass. I'm nae going to tell ye anything, so please stop asking."

Kelly pouted. As far as Braeden could tell, she'd given up for now, but she wasn't happy about it.

"Hey, Sean wants to know when you're going to come back down and practice with them. The guys really like you. They'd be good friends to have." She tipped her head waiting for him to speak.

"I havenae the time right now. Once this business is settled, I will. I promise." He checked the hallway again. "I must go. Tessa may need me."

"Or you may need her." Kelly's impish grin had returned along with her teasing. "Are you two doing it yet?"

"Doing what, lass?"

Kelly laughed at his question, or was she laughing at him? "Come on, Braeden. You know exactly what I mean. I know you're from Scotland, but I believe they even do it there." Her laughter continued and tears sprang into her eyes.

Braeden didn't know what she found so funny. He had no idea what it was he should be doing with Tessa... or did he? Finally understanding Kelly's question, Braeden's face lit up and he too began to laugh. "Kelly, ye be a nosy wench. 'Tis nae yer business, so stop yer teasing."

Kelly coughed and hiccoughed her way out of laughing. "I'm sorry. I couldn't help it. The way you look at her, the way your eyes follow her wherever she goes. You're in love with her, aren't you?"

Braeden eyed the ceiling before answering. "Aye. I am." It was the first time he'd admitted to himself.

"Do you think she loves you? You know, since the two of you have been spending so much time together. It's the perfect way to get to know someone."

"I dinnae believe she does, but I know she wants to *do it* with me as ye've said. I cannae betray John's trust. He has asked me to protect Tessa and I will, even if it means I must protect her from meself."

"Don't be silly. I'm sure John didn't have that in mind when he asked you to protect her." Kelly came around the desk to stand next to him as he peered down the hall. "What are we looking at?" She was teasing him again.

"Ye ken yer like a burr under me saddle." He teased back.

"That's not very nice. I tease out of love, Braeden." She slid her arm around his waist and rested her head on his shoulder.

Braeden felt lucky to have such a good friend and to know she loved him. "Ye ken I never had a sister, but if I had one I would want it to be ye."

"Well, I'll consider you my honorary brother, since I don't have one either."

He placed a sweet kiss on top of her head. "Mmm. What have ye used to wash yer hair? It smells good enough to eat."

Kelly giggled. "It's some strawberry-kiwi shampoo. It smells good, huh?"

"No wonder. I love strawberries." He sniffed her hair again.

"As much as you love Tessa?" She arched one eyebrow as she spun away and faced him.

"Kelly, yer relentless. I must go. Say hello to yer man fer me." He marched down the hallway before she could get another word out. He needed to be sure Tessa was alright. After all, he'd left her alone for a full five minutes, anything could have happened.

TESSA WAS GLAD to have some time alone. Having Braeden so close all the time was making her crazy. It wasn't him. It was her. She was starting to lose control of herself around him. What she'd done in the limo was embarrassing now that she thought about it. The way he'd had to remove her arms from around his waist just to get out of the car—what must he think of her? Surely in the time he came from women were more demure and reserved. She couldn't imagine them running around throwing themselves at men. She should ask him about that. She had a living, breathing Scottish history book at her disposal. There were lots of things she'd like to know. She'd make a list. That was what she did when she started to feel her life reeling out of control. She made lists. They kept her grounded and sane. She grabbed a notebook and a pen and started writing down her questions for Braeden. Then, as the door to her office opened and she saw him standing there, she crumpled the paper and threw it in the trash.

"Hi." It was all she could manage to choke out. God he was perfect. Her breathing quickened along with her racing pulse. Tessa's eyes seemed locked on his lips. She could almost taste them, could almost feel how soft and sweet they'd be. She wanted to rush to him, throwing herself into his arms, running her fingers through his curly brown locks. The angel and devil were back. The devil was telling her to do it and this time the angel agreed. That little talking to she'd had with herself had done absolutely no good whatsoever.

"Tessa," he appeared worried, but his face relaxed when he saw her. "Yer alright."

"Yes. I'm fine. Are *you* okay?" He seemed a little frazzled, which was very unlike him.

"Aye. I'm fine." He sat in the chair opposite her own, his eyes never leaving hers. What was he trying to do to her with his penetrating gaze? Whatever it was, it was working. The tingling sensation she was feeling between her thighs was getting stronger by the minute, causing her to fidget in her chair. Tessa forced herself to glance towards the window.

"When Da gets back we'll let him know Bobby will be here later. Then maybe we should get something to eat." Who was she kidding? She didn't care about food. It was Braeden she was hungry for and if he didn't make love to her soon, she was going to either make a complete and total fool of herself, or she was going to explode. Those were the only two options she could see.

Awkward silence filled the room. Tessa thought, *I should say something.* Nothing came to her. She began tapping her fingers on the desk and rearranging the sparse items on top of it. The stapler was moved from one side of the desk to the other. Her papers were neatly straightened. She spent a good amount of time lining her pen up with the top of the papers until it was just right. Finally, frustration won out and she pushed her chair back, slamming it into the wall, before rounding her desk and planting her lips square on Braeden's. His eyes went wide with surprise, before softening with desire. His hands held her face close as he responded to her kiss with moist, sensual lips and a tongue that teased its way past Tessa's lips to mingle with hers. The passionate force of their kisses shut down all of the earlier thoughts of doubt and self-consciousness that had floated through her head. All she could think was, *he wants this too.* His hands moved to her waist as he guided her onto his lap, where Tessa became extremely aware of the enormity of his desire. Breathing had become less important, all she wanted was his mouth on hers and if that meant less breathing, then so be it. She'd rather pass out in his arms than stop now. Through this haze of lust, Tessa heard an annoying buzzing sound. It happened once, twice and then a third time. She momentarily ignored it before realizing it was the intercom on her desk. She pushed back, but Braeden wasn't ready to let her go and she didn't want to stop either. The pleading in his eyes tore at her heart, but responsibility won out.

"Braeden. That's my intercom. My Da may be back. I have to see who it is." She was gasping for breath by now and stumbled back behind her desk, straightening her blouse, skirt and hair as she went. "Yes," she managed to shakily get out.

"Tessa, your father's back. He can see you now." Kelly's cheery voice came through the speaker, but was there a tinge of I-know-what-you've-been-doing in her announcement?

Braeden was busy fanning himself with his kilt, his face a combination of tortured soul meets you've-been-caught.

"We'll be right there," Tessa shouted. "Come on, Braeden. We should go."

He grunted something in response and with one last fan of his kilt, he let it settle down around him as he checked to see if everything had calmed down and then led the way to John's office.

CHAPTER *16*

OHN MCTAVISH PACED the floor of his office, stopping occasionally to gaze out the window at the glittering lights of the Las Vegas Strip.

"Tessa tells me that you'd be willing to help us, Bobby. Are you sure you wish to make your relationship with Niall any more caustic than it already is?" John turned to face Bobby, who had settled on the comfy sofa facing the windows and the million-dollar view from The Albannach.

"My relationship with Niall is nonexistent. He won't be happy to know I'm helping you, but at this point he doesn't know you're even speaking with me. He thinks he's effectively blackballed me everywhere of any significance here on The Strip." Bobby sipped the whiskey John had given him.

"The situation is fraught with danger. Two people have already died, possibly three, and I'm not sure why, but I suspect it has something to do with Niall's plans."

"What exactly are those plans?"

"I'm not sure, but I know it has something to do with Braeden's watch."

"Does the watch have some significance to Niall?"

"Well, you remember when he introduced us all to his cousin, Ian Campbell. And then Ian disappeared."

"Niall said he went back home to Scotland."

"I believe the man was Braeden's father."

"But Braeden's a MacDonald, isn't he?" Bobby appeared confused.

"Yes. He is, but despite the hatred between the two clans back in the seventeenth century, Ian fell in love with Iona, Braeden's mother, a MacDonald. They were forced to keep their relationship secret. They handfasted right under the noses of both clans. Iona became pregnant, but according to Braeden, she died when he was too young to have anything more than vague memories of her. He was raised by his grandmother. The Campbell's were most unhappy with Ian and fearing for his life, he took the watch, which has been handed down from generation to generation to the first born son of Braeden's specific Campbell line. It was rightfully Ian's and then it was passed on to Braeden. Niall had learned about the legend of the watch and he tried to track it through history, but it was lost in the late seventeenth century and now he understands why. The watch can transport the owner through time, but more importantly, if the watch is opened, it stops time. Niall thinks that because he's a Campbell, the watch belongs to him. He, of course, intends to use it for nefarious purposes."

Bobby silently pondered John's words, sipping his whiskey and gazing out the window.

"Well, we must stop him then. I know Niall Campbell all too well and he will stop at nothing to get what he wants and I suspect what he wants is to see you ruined, while he gains all of the wealth and respect he believes you've received but feels he deserves."

"I thought the same, although why he wants to destroy me is something I don't understand."

"You're one of the wealthiest men in the country, John, and your peers have a great deal of respect for you. I'm sure Niall feels slighted by the powers-that-be here in Vegas. He's aimed his wrath at you because you've just opened the hottest casino on The Strip and he's envious of that accomplishment. He'd like nothing better than to take it away from you somehow and if he can't do that, then he'll destroy what you've created and enjoy watching you fail."

DETECTIVE NANCE REQUESTED that Tessa come down to the station. He said he had some news to share with her. At their previous meeting, he'd practically accused her of killing Danny. She hoped this wasn't going to be a repeat performance.

They were greeted cordially by Detective Nance as Braeden joined her in his office. "It's good to see you both," he said.

Neither Tessa nor Braeden said a thing. Instead they waited for the detective to explain why he'd called them in.

"Miss McTavish, I owe you an apology. I know that the last time you were in here, you were a suspect in Danny's death. We've spent a good deal of time going through his home and his belongings, along with his computer and cell phone. Our technical staff managed to retrieve some interesting information from that computer and I wanted to share it with you."

Tessa scrunched her brow in suspicion. "Why?"

"Well, it would be better if you read this for yourself." He handed her a printout of a letter addressed to her. "Go ahead and read that. It will explain a lot of things."

> *Tessa, I'm writing this note to explain to you that I can't marry you. I'm sure you've received my text by now and I hope you won't be too disappointed at this news. I want you to know that I was never in love with you. It was all just a ruse. You are a very sweet person and I'm sorry that I led you on like that. I should have never been engaged to you. I'm a married man. Tanya and I have been married for a little over a year now. We kept it quiet because my manager thought it would be best not to upset my fan base.*
>
> *As for why I did it, it was because I was expected to. There is a certain man in Las Vegas who would be happy to see your father fail. He would go to any lengths to destroy him and the new hotel, and he hoped to do it through you. You wouldn't understand the reasons behind why I did what I did, so I won't go into further detail. I just wanted to apologize and to let you know that I couldn't go on lying to you. I couldn't do any of it anymore. I hope you'll forgive me. Once I tell him what I've done, I'm going to have to leave town, so you'll probably never see me again. Please be careful, I believe he will come after you to further his ends.*
>
> *Danny*

"Do you know who he's talking about?" Detective Nance took the paper from her hand. When she didn't answer right away, he continued. "It's the strangest thing I've ever seen. There were no outwards signs of trauma, the autopsy showed nothing to speak of. There were no drugs in his system. It was as if the life was just drained from his body. I still can't believe it. We couldn't find any reason he should be dead. Same thing with that other guy. The one who worked at The Albannach. Once we found out Danny was married, we got in touch with his wife. She hasn't been able to tell us anything about who this man Danny spoke of could be. We're completely stumped, so if there's anything you might be able to tell us, it would be appreciated."

"Nothing comes to mind at the moment, I'm still a little shocked by the note. If I can think of anything at all, I'll be sure to call you right away."

"Thank you, Miss McTavish. We'd appreciate it."

OUTSIDE OF THE police station, Tessa stopped dead in her tracks and faced Braeden. She didn't have to say anything at all. He understood and wrapped his arms around her in the hug she needed.

"Why didnae ye tell him about Campbell?" Braeden wondered.

"I don't know. Something inside of me thought it might not be the best idea. I'd hate for any other innocent victims to fall into his web."

"We've got to stop him. Yer father met with Bobby. Has he mentioned anything to ye?"

"Not yet. He'll be interested to hear about this though. We're all going to have to be extremely careful around Niall. If he's capable of killing Danny and Kenneth, and leaving no trace that would lead to him as a suspect, then anything is possible."

"We'd best be careful then. He won't get away with this." Braeden was sure of that. He'd see to it that this particular Campbell paid for his misdeeds. He held Tessa away from him and looked deeply into her eyes. "I willnae let anything happen to ye, Tessa. I promise."

"I know you won't, Braeden. I'm not going to let anything happen to you either." She smiled brightly at him to let him know she was okay.

Braeden had to chuckle at this feisty woman who wanted to protect him too.

"Are you laughing at me because you don't think I can do it?" Tessa asked as she gave him a challenging look.

"Nae. Actually, I believe ye could protect me and do a verra good job of it. Of course, I don't know where yer protection specialties lie." He winked and chucked her under the chin.

"You'll see. If the time ever comes where I need to step up and save your ass, I will do an excellent job of it. I promise."

"I've nae doubt."

THERE WAS A wedding taking place at the resort on this particular Saturday. Tessa was all over the grounds, making sure that everything was perfect for this special occasion. The bride looked gorgeous in her Scottish wedding gown, draped with her husband's tartan. The Scottish-themed weddings they were specializing in here at The Albannach were drawing a lot of attention from couples seeking to honor their Scottish heritage. There were bagpipers who'd been employed to play both be-fore and after the ceremony. The benches the guests would sit on were festooned with the family tartan and flowers that included the Scottish thistle as their main component. Everything down to the bride's bou-quet had been carefully planned for today's big event. Tessa was excited. She'd already been hard at work planning weddings at the resort, but this was her first solo attempt at being a wedding planner and things seemed to be going really well. She mentally high-fived herself on her accomplishment.

The wedding chapel and reception hall were located in a separate area of the resort, so that the couple and their guests got the feel of being at their own private Scottish castle. The suite the couple would use after the wedding was also Tessa's design. They were going to love all the special touches she had incorporated into the room. Tessa loved romance and she let it shine through in her wedding design.

"Tessa, everything is beyond our expectations," the mother of the bride gushed upon seeing the chapel that morning. "Julia is going to be so thrilled with all of this."

"I'm so happy you're happy," Tessa said, laying a hand on Mrs. Timmons' arm. "Have you seen your corsage yet?"

"No, can I?"

"Of course, you wait right here and I'll bring it to you."

Tessa went into the kitchen of the banquet facility and removed a beautiful box from the refrigerator. She peeked inside and smiled at the lovely flowers her friend Emily, the resort florist, had put together for the mothers of the bride and groom. Heading back out she waved to Braeden who was standing in the shade of the building, watching her every move. She really did feel so much safer when he was around.

He smiled and waved back, setting her heart aflutter. She was so focused on him that she nearly tripped over her own two feet.

"Are you alright, Tessa?" Mrs. Timmons asked. "Fine, just a little clumsy." She smiled reassuringly.

"I thought it might have something to do with that handsome young man over there." She nodded in Braeden's direction. "He hasn't taken his eyes off of you for a moment." She sighed and held her hands to her heart. "So sweet. And romantic."

"He's supposed to keep an eye on me. He's just doing his job, Mrs. Timmons."

"I don't know about that, but there seems to be more to the way he's looking at you than just concern for your well being. It's almost… dare I say it, lustful." She glanced Braeden's way again and he winked and nodded in her direction, prompting Mrs. Timmons to fan herself.

"Oh, my! He's very handsome, Tessa. If I wasn't an old married lady, I'd certainly set my sights on him."

Tessa surreptitiously eyed Braeden as he stood holding up the wall and looking as tall, dark and handsome as ever. She decided it was time to change the subject. "Here's the corsage. What do you think?"

"Oh my, it's beautiful. I can hardly wait to get dressed so I can put it on."

"Good. My friend Emily made identical corsages for you and Mrs. Johnson. I thought they were lovely, but it's always good to know that the person who's going to wear it loves it too."

"I do. I love everything about this. My grandparents were from Scotland and they would have loved this." Tears sprang to her eyes and she quickly brushed them away. "You'll have to excuse me. I'm a little emotional today."

"Perfectly understandable. Now, if you'll excuse me, I've still got a lot of items to check off my list and you need to get dressed for the photos. I'll see you later at the wedding and if there's anything you need in the meantime, just let me know."

"I will and thank you again."

Tessa waved Braeden away from his post and he followed her as she went to the aviary to speak with the falconer about having two of their beautiful hawks available for the wedding.

"I think we'll have Jossy and Joe attend the wedding," Terrence the falconer was a great asset to the resort. He not only cared for all of the birds, but he led classes for those who wished to learn about birds of prey and falconry.

"That will be perfect. You're sure they'll behave themselves." Tessa was a little nervous about including them in the wedding plans, but Amanda and James insisted they wanted them.

"They'll behave. You can be sure of it." Terrence gazed over to the two birds who sat perched high atop their enclosure.

Knowing Terrence, Tessa didn't question it any further. He was a master with the birds and she admired his dedication to his art. Tessa had always been a huge fan of birds of prey. They were majestic creatures and she could spend all day watching them. She'd taken some falconry lessons from Terrence and felt pretty secure in handling them.

Another item checked off the list and Tessa was on to the kitchen, where she met with Chef Navarro about the food that would be served before and during the reception. She checked in on the dining area and couldn't believe her eyes. Everything was beyond amazing. Rustic tables and chairs were covered with beautiful white silk tablecloths, their brocade pattern depicting thistles, topped with a combination of burlap and tartan. Candles were everywhere along with more of the beautiful flower creations from Emily. She couldn't have wished for anything better. As a matter of fact, if this had been for her wedding, she would have been thrilled. The thought that she should have been getting married here in another month didn't faze Tessa one bit. She didn't regret the fact that she wouldn't be a bride. How could she? She hadn't loved Danny at all, he hadn't loved her, he was already married and the whole proposal had been the villainous scheme of the man she now considered her enemy. Her only regret was that Danny couldn't be saved from Niall Campbell and she vowed that she would see to it that Niall paid for what he'd done.

Next stop was the bridal chamber. The cleaning staff had done a stellar job of making the room, fashioned after a sixteenth-century Scottish laird's room, as beautiful as could be. The large four-poster bed, covered with silk brocade bedding, was just as she wanted it—romantic and inviting. The fireplace was ready to go at a moment's notice. Like the other fireplaces in the hotel, it was not there to keep anyone warm, but it did add ambience for a romantic evening. Bobby spelled the candles, so they would light up just before the bride and groom came back to their suite.

Everything was ready for a romantic bath for the happy couple. The tub was large enough for two and the room itself exuded old-world charm in a modern setting. The stone walls and floors rather than being cold, created a warmth enhanced by more candles, flowers, sweet smelling soaps, beautiful fixtures and more. A bucket for icing the champagne completed the scene.

Just a few more hours and The Albannach would be on its way to hosting another very special wedding. Tessa couldn't be more excited.

"You are glowing today, Tessa." Braeden's soft, deep voice sounded next to her ear. She'd almost forgotten he was there as he'd silently stayed out of her way while she made sure every detail of this wedding was perfect. She turned quickly and found herself looking directly at his chest. She took a step back and stumbled. Braeden quickly wrapped an arm around her waist, holding her in place. She could feel the warm tickle of his breath on her cheek as he bent his head lower to whisper in her ear. "So, so beautiful."

She couldn't feel her legs beneath her as her heart pounded in her chest and her brain seemed to shut down. She couldn't think what to do, so she simply stayed where she was, drinking in the feel of him and the scent of him. He'd discovered cologne since he'd been here and she loved whatever it was he was wearing. The girls at The Scented Male had given him a complimentary bottle of a blend they were calling

Braeden. She breathed it in deeply, closing her eyes and savoring the moment. He'd turned the tables on her. Wasn't he the one who said he couldn't betray her father's trust?

"Braeden…"

His lips traced a path from her ear to her lips, gently kissing them and leaving her shaking in their wake.

"I want you, Tessa. I can't deny it."

"But, my father. You said…"

"I ken what I said, but I dinnae believe I can keep my word. Not after what happened in yer office."

"You're not breaking your word. You're still protecting me." She wanted him too and she had to make him see that he wouldn't be betraying her father's trust.

"And who's protecting ye from me, lass?"

The only response Tessa had was to kiss him back and it led to one of those kisses she'd remember for the rest of her life. She'd never been kissed like this before. His lips were soft on hers, yet demanding. He held her head in place with one hand, while the other traced a path down the center of her back and then to her hips, drawing her even closer. There was now not an inch of space between them. Their bodies were touching completely and Tessa felt as though she might be absorbed right into him. She dropped her checklist and vaguely heard it scatter across the floor. Her mind kept telling her that this wasn't the time or the place for this, but her body betrayed her by molding itself to Braeden's, enjoying the feel of his hard chest and strong arms. Her hands seemed to move of their own accord, feeling that chest, those shoulders and then around to his broad, well-muscled back and down to his strong, rounded buttocks. His hands were everywhere now. One moment cupping her breasts and then the next traveling up her thigh beneath her skirt. His sure fingers found their way up to her panties and, pushing them aside, he proceeded to probe her moist center. Her heart pounded in her chest as she hung on to him, afraid that if she let go he would disappear and she'd be left wanting what he was offering, but only on the brink of receiving it.

"You want me lass. I can feel ye. Yer ready fer me." Braeden continued ministering to her swollen sheath. "Tell me ye want me, Tessa. Tell me."

She was floating on a hot, horny cloud of wanting him. "Yes. I want you. Mmmm…" She was about to reach her peak when her brain and her damned sense of responsibility kicked back into gear. "Braeden, we can't do this," she rasped out. "There's a wedding happening in a couple of hours and this room is meant for the bride and groom, not for us."

He reluctantly removed his fingers, leaving Tessa feeling hollow and lost. "Not today perhaps, but soon." His husky voice sent shivers throughout her body as she pushed herself away from him.

"Yes. Soon." She quickly kissed his lips one last time and then before she could change her mind and indulge any further, she stepped away from him, once again adjusting her clothing. She took a quick peek in the mirror before exiting and satisfied that she didn't look too rumpled, headed out the door.

Braeden bent down to pick up her papers and followed after her.

CHAPTER 17

THE WEDDING WENT off without a hitch and a very happy Bride and Groom enjoyed everything about it. They danced for hours with their guests, enjoyed a delicious meal and much champagne and then enjoyed the romance of the wedding suite.

John was pleased that everything had gone so smoothly and he was exceedingly proud of Tessa, telling her so when she came down to the kitchen next morning.

"Tessa, I am the proudest father in all the world. You are truly the best thing that has ever happened to me. I don't know what I'd do without you." He kissed the top of her head and pulled her into a warm hug.

"Thank you, Da. I've enjoyed every minute of it. We're all booked up for the coming year. I'm excited to be able to help these couples plan their perfect wedding."

"I only wish your Mother could be here to see what a lovely young woman you've become." He held her away from himself to look into her eyes.

Tessa smiled sadly. "I know. I miss her too, Da."

"And what about you my darling. What romance is in your future?"

Tessa blushed. She wasn't used to discussing these things with her father, but she wanted him to know that she had developed feelings for Braeden. "Well, Da, if you must know." She averted her eyes momentarily and then decided he had a right to know how happy she was feeling. "I believe I've found someone."

"I can see he makes you happy and that makes me happy. When do I get to meet the lucky man."

"You already know him."

"I do. Who could it be?" The glint of mischief in John's eyes led Tessa to believe that he may have been on to them all along.

"Who do you think it is?"

John was obviously going to have fun teasing Tessa as he named every man— young, old or even married—who worked at the casino. "It's none of them. I can hardly believe it. That only leaves one that I can think of." He looked skywards as if he were thinking of more names.

Tessa jumped in before he could continue. "It's Braeden, Da."

"I thought as much. I was hoping the two of you would hit it off and I'm happy to see that I was right."

"There's just one problem."

"What would that be?"

"Braeden thinks that he'd be betraying your trust if we had any sort of relationship outside of him protecting me."

John shook his head and was about to speak when the sound of a door closing upstairs caught his attention. "We'll speak more on this later."

They waited at the kitchen counter for Braeden to make an appearance and when he did, he obviously had something on his mind. "Tessa, I'd speak with yer father for a moment. Alone, please."

Tessa tipped her head and gazed questioningly at him. "Sure. I'll be in the living room if you need me." *Listening to every word.*

BRAEDEN WAITED FOR her to leave the room before he spoke. "John, I have something I must say and I hope that you'll give me your blessing."

"What could it be, Braeden? You seem so serious."

"Well, sir, I believe I'm falling in love with Tessa. I've told her it could never be because…"

"Because why, Braeden? Surely you don't think I'd object."

"I understand if you don't think I'm the man fer yer daughter…"

"Stop. I do think you're the man for my Tessa. I've been hoping you'd see that too. Now, that doesn't mean you're not expected to do your job. I still need you to protect her, especially now with everything that's happened."

The nervous energy Braeden had been feeling was about to bubble over, but he maintained his serious demeanor. "Of course. It is my honor and privilege to see that she's safe."

"Good. Now go tell her the good news."

Tessa came flying back into the room and into Braeden's arms. She kissed him soundly on the lips. "I heard every word. I wasn't sure you'd ever broach the subject with him, but you did." She was obviously happy and so was Braeden, who let down his guard and smiled broadly at

John and then kissed Tessa, picking her up and swinging her around in a circle before putting her down.

"Alright you two. Back to work with you. This hotel isn't going to run itself now, is it?"

PATROLLING THE CASINO floor with Tessa by his side, Braeden was happy beyond words. This flaxen-haired beauty, that he'd admired from the first moment he laid eyes on her, was to be his. He was a verra lucky man. He'd escaped death in his own time and been transported to this very hotel by the watch his Grannie had given him. Was it fate that brought him to this place, to this time, to this woman? He believed it must be. But there was still one thing standing in the way of their future and his name was Niall Campbell. He'd need to be dealt with and soon, before he did any more damage or murdered anymore victims.

Tessa seemed to read his mind. "What are we going to do about Niall?"

"We should talk to Bobby again and then perhaps Bobby and I should pay a visit to Campbell."

"I'm going with you."

"I dinnae believe that to be wise, Tessa. Campbell is a dangerous man and there's no telling what he'll do."

"I know, but if you remember correctly, I promised to protect you and if Niall Campbell intends to harm you in any way, I want to be there so I can stop him."

"Tessa…"

"Shhh! Don't argue this one with me. You won't win. I'm going and that's all there is to it."

Braeden admired her spunk, but he also feared for her safety. Everything in him told him not to bring her along, but how was he going to get away without her knowing. He was supposed to follow her everywhere she went. He'd come up with a plan later, but for now they needed to meet with Bobby again.

"Before we do anything else, I think we should celebrate." Tessa was eyeing him with a seductive expression on her face.

"What did ye have in mind, love?"

"Love! You called me love. I like that. Let's go back to our house and maybe lay out by the pool for a while. I'll put a call in to Bobby and ask him to meet us here when he can."

"I've seen the people sitting out at the pool. I don't have one of those bathing suits they wear."

"You don't need one. It's just going to be the two of us."

A slow smile made its way across his lips as he snaked an arm around Tessa's waist and pulled her to him. "Yer trying to tempt me, lass."

"And what if I am?" Tessa teased.

"I'm all for it." Braeden dipped his head and teased her lips with his tongue before settling an impassioned kiss on her lips, leaving her breathless.

"Now who's tempting who?"

Braeden chuckled. "Let's go. Me kilt isnae verra good at hiding me feelings fer ye."

"We may need to get you some pants." She eyed his kilt, honing in on the tent sprouting up in front of him. "Maybe not. I like knowing what you're thinking." Tessa laughed and took his hand as the two of them hurried through the casino into the private McTavish compound.

ALONE AT LAST and knowing that they weren't betraying anyone's trust, Braeden swept Tessa into his arms, carrying her to the pool area, where he plopped them both down on the large mattress inside the cabana. For a long moment he did nothing more than gaze at this lovely angel. He hadn't known her before his arrival in this time and now he couldn't imagine spending another moment without her in his life. He wanted to make this moment last for as long as possible. John wasn't expected back for some time. He was meeting with his hotel managers to go over issues that had cropped up since the grand opening, so there was no fear he would interrupt them yet again.

"Tessa, do ye have one of those things I see the women at the pool wearing?" He eyed her with a bit of mischief.

"You mean a bikini?"

"Aye. Is that what ye call it?"

Tessa nodded. "I was going to go get changed. You know, to be more comfortable."

"Ye should do that. I'll wait fer ye here."

"Do you want me to see if my father has a bathing suit you could wear, although I don't see how it would fit you."

"Nae. I'll be fine as I am." He lay back on the mattress, feeling quite at home and ready to make Tessa his.

℘

"I'LL BE RIGHT BACK." Tessa thought they'd be making love by now. She wasn't sure what Braeden was up to, but she'd go along with it if it meant he'd make her feel the way he had in the bathroom of the bridal suite. She was getting herself all worked up just thinking about it.

She went to her room and found her skimpiest bikini and put it on. She admired herself in the mirror before heading back downstairs to the kitchen where she loaded a tray with a pitcher of lemonade, glasses and a plate of fruit, cheese and crackers. Humming to herself she made her way back outside to Braeden, who lay in all his glory, stark naked on the mattress. The sight of him took her breath away. He was like a glorious marble sculpture, perfect in every way. He'd swept his shoulder-length curly locks back from his face and secured it with a leather thong. *It won't be staying that way for long,* she thought. She wanted to run her fingers through his dark brown tresses. She took her time approaching. He was unaware of her as he lounged, eyes closed and enjoying the heat, maybe for the first time since he'd been here. She examined every part of him—strong chest and arms, his chiseled abs and the vee that led to...

He opened his eyes, apparently sensing her presence. "Tessa, yer back. I think I fell asleep. I dreamed of ye."

The intensity of those eyes, taking her in as she approached, made her a bit wobbly on her feet. *Breathe. Breathe. You're almost there.* Placing the tray on a nearby table, she slowly stripped off her cover up to reveal the tiny bathing suit she'd chosen just for him. Its bright blue hue matched the color of her eyes and left little to the imagination.

Braeden reached out a hand for her to take and turned her so he could take in all there was to see. He undid the strings holding the bathing suit in place and stripped her of it, cradling her bottom as he drew her in closer and closer. Now sitting up, he pulled her in between his legs. Gazing up at her, his tongue flicked her navel and a slow, seductive smile spread across his lips. This slow motion torture was getting to Tessa in the best possible way.

Tessa placed her hands on his shoulders, pressing him back onto the mattress, where she sat astride his belly. She wanted him inside of her, but she'd decided to go at his pace. So far he'd been masterful at turning her on and she couldn't wait to experience all that Braeden MacDonald could give her.

Braeden reached up and cupped her breasts, massaging them with his fingers and pinching her pebbled nipples. A moan of ecstasy escaped her lips as he sat up and captured one pearly gem in his mouth. The sensation of his warm mouth and slick tongue alone, as he played with her nipples, almost brought her to climax. She rubbed her now dripping hot slit along his abdomen before raising it and moving to rub on his cock. She loved the feel of him, rock hard and throbbing for her. Her mind was overcome with the sensations assailing her from all parts of her body, when Braeden suddenly picked her up and brought her down on his shaft. Her eyes flew open in surprise as she sat completely still for a moment, enjoying the feel of him inside of her.

Slowly she began to move on him. A sensual, rhythmic dance had begun, leisurely at first and then as Braeden grasped onto her hips, helping her move with him, their pace quickening with each thrust. Arching her back, Tessa pushed her breasts forward inviting Braeden to take them into his mouth again, which he did with wanton enthusiasm. Sweat dripped from both their bodies, the external heat adding to the fire burning within Tessa. Braeden's eyes were locked on hers. She licked her parched lips. His response was to flip her onto her back and take her mouth in a hot, demanding kiss, his tongue plundering her mouth as his manhood plundered her sheath. Her whole body thrummed with the feel of him in her, on her. Sublime sensations stole her breath away as they built to the point of no return and her walls convulsed with pleasure as Braeden joined her, both of them crying out as he spilled his seed.

Panting in each other's arms, they allowed the after-effects of their lovemaking to wash over them. Tessa could hardly gather the strength to speak, so instead she closed her eyes and drifted off to sleep.

SHE SLEPT SWEETLY nestled with her back against him. He woke with thoughts of taking her again. His lips gently kissed the back of her shoulder, causing her to stretch and open her eyes.

She turned in his arms to face him. "You're amazing," was her simple statement. He had no other response than to softly kiss her inviting lips. In all his years and of all the women he'd known, Tessa was unlike anyone of them. She was a rare gem and yet as unlikely as it seemed, he'd found her and was lucky enough to make her his own.

"Let's go in the pool." Tessa gazed lovingly up at him.

He could find no reason to disagree with her. It was hotter now than he'd noticed before, but perhaps that was because he'd been too busy to take note.

Tessa rose and pulled him up to join her. "Come on." She let go of his hand and dove into the turquoise blue waters. He'd never been in a pool before, having always swum in the loch near his home. This was completely new to him, but also completely pleasurable. He swam below the surface of the water, amazed at its clarity. He caught Tessa around the waist and pulled her to him. The sweat was now washed from their bodies, but the water provided them with another sensation. Cool and refreshing, it gave Braeden a renewed desire to explore Tessa's rapturous body once again and from the lust he saw in her eyes, she was more than ready for him.

Glancing around the pool, he noted the wide steps leading up and out of the water. The shallowness there would be perfect for what he had planned. Holding Tessa close he ran his hand between her legs, loving the feel of her and the way she laid back in the water, eyes closed, a rapturous smile on her face. His thumb found the little nub he knew would bring her much pleasure and he played it, never taking his eyes from her face. The sight of her being pleasured by him had his cock throbbing. Wrapping an arm around her waist, he swam with her back to the steps. She laid back, open for him and he lifted her sweet bottom from beneath the water, up to meet his hungry tongue so he could devour her swollen entrance. Sounds of pure bliss escaped Tessa's lips and so he continued, knowing he could bring her to climax this way over and over if he wanted, and he did want to. She cried out and squirmed in his arms, but he held her fast as wave after wave of ecstasy exploded through her. Braeden flipped her onto her stomach and Tessa rested on her elbows, her bottom in the air. Her center beckoned Braeden to fill her to the hilt with his engorged shaft, which he did, growling as he watched her from above. He gathered her hair away from her face, pulling her head back so he could see her eyes. She stared back at him, challenging him and he met that challenge, driving himself into her over and over until he cried out with his own release, while at the same time feeling Tessa's core convulsing around him in its own eruption of pleasure.

EMERGING FROM THE pool, Tessa grabbed some towels she'd placed nearby. They dried themselves off and then went back to the cabana, where she poured them both some warm lemonade.

She took a sip and made a face that caused Braeden to laugh at her silliness. "Needs ice," she said. "And none of this food is good anymore.

Let's go get dressed and then grab some food."

"Aye. I'm hungry." Braeden rubbed his belly.

"You're always hungry," Tessa said. A huge smile had been plastered on her face all afternoon. She was so ecstatic she thought she'd burst. "I don't know that anyone has a right to be this happy."

"Ye do, Tessa." Braeden grabbed the tray of food and kissed the top of her head, making his way to the cottage.

Tessa was hot on his heels. "You do too, Braeden. I can't think of anyone who deserves it more than you." She smiled up at him as he waited for her at the door. "I can't wait for all of this drama to be over so we can have a normal life."

"Where are we to meet Bobby?" he asked.

"At the club, but not until later. He'll meet us after his show, so we have plenty of time to have something to eat and then maybe take a little nap."

"I like that idea." They were inside now and Braeden placed the tray on the kitchen counter.

"I like it, too." Tessa got serious for a moment. She wrapped her arms around Braeden's waist and gazed up at him. "I love you, Braeden MacDonald."

"And I love ye, Tessa McTavish."

CHAPTER 18

THE CORNER OF the club where they chose to meet with Bobby was dark, lit by a single candle in the center of the table. The perfect place for a romantic interlude, or for planning your next move in a dangerous game of chess.

Tessa held tightly to Braeden's hand as they waited. "What's taking him so long?" The thumping of the music and the voices of the club patrons were raised in celebratory glee. What everyone was celebrating was anyone's guess. It could simply be that they were in Las Vegas and they were having fun.

"Dinnae fear, Tessa. He'll be here." She could see that Braeden was doing his best to reassure her, but it was obvious that he was just as worried as she was. Time was ticking by and it was now an hour past their appointed meeting time.

A server came by their table with an envelope in hand. "I was told to give this to you, Miss McTavish."

"Thank you. I'm afraid I don't know your name. I've tried to meet everyone who works here, but it's been impossible."

"Cassie." The young woman offered. I've only been here for a couple of days.

"I'm pleased to meet you, Cassie. Is that short for Cassandra?"

"No. Don't laugh, but it's short for Cassiopeia." She fixed the napkins on her tray.

"Your parents named you after the constellation." Tessa liked to get to know the employees at the hotel and engaging them in conversation was one way she liked to do it. She knew she wouldn't forget this cocktail waitress's name now.

"No, some character on a SciFi TV show they used to watch." She snickered at that. "I can't remember the name of it though."

"Well, Cassie, I hope you'll be happy here with us."

"I'm sure I will. Can I get you a drink or something to eat?"

"No, thank you. We're waiting for someone." The girl began walking away, but Tessa stopped her. "Who gave this to you?"

"Some man by the door. He didn't say who he was. I can try to find him for you, if you like."

"No. That's okay. Thanks again, Cassie."

Tessa glanced down at the envelope in her hand and her heart sank. She didn't think this was going to be a good thing. She raised her eyes to Braeden's and he appeared as worried as she did.

"Open it, lass." Braeden was scanning the room; she assumed he was trying to find the man in question.

The envelope was made of a heavyweight paper and appeared to be very old. Upon opening it and removing the paper inside, she found it to be of the same quality. She wished she had more light, so she could get a better look at it. As it was, she held it close to the candle and read.

Bobby is with us and unless you'd like to see the same thing happen to him that befell our friends Danny and Kenneth, you'd best join me at The Las Vegas Society of Magick and Sorcery. Don't tell anyone where you're going and you'd best move quickly. Bobby doesn't have much time left.

Tessa was just thinking this was the piece of evidence she needed for the police, when the paper flared up in her hands and disappeared.

"We'd better hurry. Bobby needs us." Tessa grabbed her purse and headed for the door. She didn't get far before Braeden reached her and pulled her to a stop.

"You can't go. It's too dangerous."

"The letter was sent to me. If I don't go, they'll kill Bobby."

"No matter. I cannae allow you to put yourself in danger like this."

"You can't allow it!" Tessa's stubborn streak arose and she narrowed her eyes at him. "You can't tell me what to do and if you remember correctly, you're job is to stay with me. You can't go without me." She was feeling triumphant. There was no way he could argue with her on that one.

Braeden sighed in resignation. "We should at least let your father know what's going on."

"I don't think that's a good idea. I don't want my father to be in danger. If this is Niall Campbell we're dealing with, and I'm pretty sure it is, he's had it in for my father for as long as I can remember."

"I thought they had a cordial relationship."

"Just because he stops by and is as nice as pie, doesn't mean a thing. He's always poking around to see what my father's doing and then he goes off and tries to disrupt it. Braeden, we don't have time to stand here arguing about this, we've got to help Bobby."

Braeden nodded and took her by the hand, leading her through the crowds of people on the dance floor and out through the doors of the club to the elevators.

§o

ONCE AGAIN BRAEDEN found himself in that infernal room that moved between the floors of the hotel. Tessa called it an elevator. He didn't know how it worked and that made him suspicious of it. He understood its purpose. The upper floors of the hotel were not easily accessed by the stairs. It's not that you couldn't use them if you wanted to, it was just that it would be an exhausting task for anyone and from what he'd seen since he'd been here, people in this century were what he would consider lazy. Yes, they got places faster and were able to accomplish tasks with lightning speed, but he found it all a bit too much. In his time, he walked or rode a horse everywhere and if he wished to speak to a friend, he would send a messenger or he would travel to see them. Everything moved at a much slower pace and he found that he missed it.

Tessa led the way to the parking garage and to a waiting car. She thanked the valet and got in the driver's seat. Braeden stood there unsure of what to do. To this point, every time they'd gone anywhere they'd gone in the limo. He cautiously got into the front seat next to Tessa, who greeted him with a reassuring smile. "Don't worry. I've been driving since I was sixteen. You might want to put your seatbelt on though." She reached across him and grabbed something which she clicked in place, effectively trapping him against the seat. She pulled out of the garage and onto Las Vegas Boulevard. The traffic was heavy and slow.

"We're going to take the next major street and use the backroads. Too much traffic." She skillfully maneuvered her way through the traffic and around the other cars. Braeden was impressed with her ability to drive. He wanted to learn this skill.

"Tessa, can ye teach me to do this?"

"I can. You'd like to learn, huh?" She didn't take her eyes from the road as she spoke with him. Her powers of concentration were admirable. Before long they were out of the crowds and onto a darkened street, devoid of cars. They drove for a while before they came to the pink stucco building with the massive white columns. "We're here." Tessa parked the car and they sat in silence, not sure what to do. "We should probably go in. Are you ready for this?"

"Aye. I've me sword and me dirk is hidden in me boots."

"Let's go then." Tessa opened the door and stepped out and Braeden hurried to do the same, but couldn't figure out how to release the seat belt. Voices behind the car had him frantic to release himself. He could hear Tessa's voice raised in anger. He had to get out. Not knowing what else to do, he removed his dirk and cut his way through the belt that held him in. Finally able to extricate himself from the car, he watched as two men led Tessa away. He followed silently, knowing that it was important to remain free if he was to help Tessa and Bobby. The men led Tessa up the stairs and into the Society building, closing the doors behind them.

Braeden stood listening at the door, but he couldn't hear a thing. He tried the door handle, but it didn't budge. It must be locked from the inside. He carefully made his way around to the side of the building in search of another door or an open window that he could crawl through. Luck didn't seem to be with him, but he continued on to the back of the building where he saw Margaret Camden exit. She didn't see him as he ducked behind some trash bins. As he watched, she swung the door to shut it, but it remained ajar as she headed across the back lot to her car. He waited while she drove away. He'd been right about Margaret from the start. He was a good judge of character and there was something about her that hadn't sat right with him from the moment he first met her. He'd shared his concerns with John and knew that they were keeping an eye on her at The Albannach. When she was out of sight, Braeden took that opportunity to hurry silently into the building.

Once inside, he wasn't sure where to go, so he stopped and listened. The sounds of voices drew him to a room off to his right. Niall's drawing room. Reaching the door, he stood outside and listened once again. This time he could hear Niall Campbell speaking. Bobby's voice rose and he heard Tessa cry out. Not waiting for an invitation, Braeden flung the door open and entered, sword in hand and ready to take on anyone who came between him and Tessa.

"Mr. MacDonald, we were waiting for ye. I was just asking Tessa where ye were. I assumed ye'd be along shortly considering that ye've been following her everywhere since yer arrival." Niall had a wand of some sort pointed at Bobby, who sat tied to a chair. "Ye're just the person I wanted to see. Ye have something I want and I think ye'll give it to me."

"Why would ye think I'd give ye anything, Campbell?"

"Because if ye don't, our friends Bobby and Tessa will come to an untimely end. Ye wouldn't want that now would ye?"

Braeden's jaw muscles clenched and unclenched as anger welled up inside of him. He knew better than to give in to it. He could defeat

Campbell. He only need wait for the right moment.

Niall Campbell shoved Tessa towards Bobby, who sat helplessly in the chair. His arms and hands were bound so that he was unable to cast any magick to help them.

"Yer sword will be of no use against my magick, so ye see ye have little choice but to cooperate with me."

Braeden moved to Tessa and Bobby. "Don't give it to him." Tessa was adamant and Bobby nodded in agreement.

"If you give it to him, we'll all be doomed anyway. He'll see to it that none of us are around to stop him from what he wishes to do."

"I asked ye once before and I'm asking ye again. What do ye want with the watch?" Braeden wasn't afraid of this sorcerer. He'd outsmart him yet.

"It will be most beneficial to me in my endeavors here in Las Vegas. I plan to use it to stop time and to rob as many casinos as possible before escaping to a safe destination where I can live in luxury for all of my days."

"Ye ken it can only be used once every twelve years. I just used it on my journey to this time. It will do ye no good."

"I know that, but what kind of sorcerer would I be if I couldn't get it to work."

"A poor excuse for one, I say." Bobby was obviously trying to antagonize him.

Niall ignored him. "If nothing else, I can still stop time with it, which will allow me to rob the casinos. I'm especially interested in the vault at The Albannach."

"Niall, you have no idea what will happen if you open that watch." Bobby eyed Braeden as he moved closer.

"Well, if ye know, perhaps ye'll tell me." Niall walked towards Bobby, waving his wand in his face.

"You'd be the last person I'd tell," Bobby snapped.

Niall laughed and turned back to Braeden. "Give me the watch, MacDonald or ye'll watch these two die."

Braeden had a plan in mind and he hoped that it would work, because if it didn't he would surely end up dead, as would Tessa and Bobby. He could hear Bobby's voice in his head, instructing him.

"Fine. Ye win. If ye wish to have the watch, I'll happily hand it over to ye, if ye promise me you'll let Tessa and Bobby live. Ye can kill me. I dinnae care. By all rights, I should be dead right now anyway."

"No." Tessa cried out. "Braeden don't give it to him."

Niall smugly mulled this over. Braeden knew that no matter what Niall agreed to, he was not planning to let any of them live.

"Alright. Ye've got a deal. Now the watch, if ye don't mind." He held out his hand to receive it.

Braeden moved as close as possible to Bobby and Tessa. Tessa moved closer and Braeden leaned down to kiss her cheek. As he did he whispered, "Hold on to me and don't let go." He reached one hand in his sporran, catching Niall's attention as he removed the watch and the other hand clasped onto Bobby while Tessa latched onto the same arm. He held the watch close to his chest before opening it and freezing time. He couldn't believe he'd actually done it.

The shocked expression, frozen as it was on Niall's face, was almost comical.

"It worked," Tessa shouted. "Now what."

"This is only going to hold them for a very brief time. As soon as ye close the watch time will start up where it left off. Untie me, please." Bobby continued speaking as they worked on his bonds. They were too difficult to untie, so Braeden used his dirk to cut through them.

"We'll need to get away for some time. We can go back to yer time, Braeden. There we can plan our next move."

"But the watch willnae work, Bobby."

"It will. I've got just the spell to get the hands to move all the way around the face, allowing us to travel."

"Okay. Let's do it." Tessa said. Her adventurous spirit was one of the things Braeden loved about her.

While Braeden and Tessa waited, Bobby invoked his incantation. They were mesmerized as they watched the hands of the dial make their way from one to twelve.

"There. It's done." From the looks of him, Bobby was quite proud of himself, as well he should be. "Close the watch and get ready to make your wish, Braeden. Let's all hold on to each other. They stood in a circle, holding each other as Braeden closed the watch and Niall and his associates came back to life.

Anger flared in Niall's eyes as he noted the three standing together. "Get them," he shouted.

Before anyone could move, Braeden wished to go back to his home and his Grannie.

Niall tried once more to stop them, but this time he used new bait. "Yerr mother will be so disappointed to have missed ye, Braeden."

Those were the last words that Braeden heard as the three of them cascaded through time, everything going black as they headed on their way to Scotland and his Grannie.

CHAPTER 19

"BRAEDEN, WAKE UP!" The sound of his Grannie's voice reached him, pulling him from the deep sleep he found himself in. Had this all been a dream? What of Tessa? And Bobby?

"Grannie," he croaked as he opened his eyes to see her concerned face staring down at him.

"Is he awake?" Was that Tessa he heard? He lifted his head and saw her smiling face. He could have wept with relief, but he kept his emotions in check.

"It looks like he is." Bobby stood close by Tessa's side.

He'd done it. He'd managed to transport the three of them from Las Vegas to Scotland and no one seemed the worse for wear, except him. He had a nasty headache, which must have been the result of their travel. The first time he'd gone alone and he'd arrived in Las Vegas unscathed. This time he hadn't been quite as fortunate. He must have hit his head when they arrived, which would account for the fact that he had somehow passed out.

"Is everyone well?" He asked, although from what he could see, they were.

"Braeden, why are ye back? And why did ye bring these poor folks with ye?" If his Grannie was surprised to see him, she was doing a very good job of hiding it.

"'Tis a long story, Grannie. They were in danger from a man who wants my watch." Braeden stood and shook the cobwebs from his brain. He hadn't thought this cottage small before, but now, after being in Las Vegas, he realized how wee it really was.

"Nae for good reasons I imagine." Esther move through the tiny room with ease and headed to her kitchen.

"Nae." Braeden confirmed her suspicions.

"I'll fix us all some food and ye can tell me all about the meadows. That is where ye went, aye?" She gathered plates, utensils and cups as she spoke.

"Aye. 'Tis. Though there be no meadows there."

"Is that the truth?" She stopped what she was doing on hearing this—her eyes were wide and her mouth agape.

"Aye. Ye would never believe it if I were to tell ye of this wondrous place I've been."

"Can I help you with anything?" Bobby asked.

"Nae. Sit where ye are and rest. I can tell ye've all been through a terrible ordeal." Esther set everything on the table and then headed back to the kitchen.

"Grannie, I fear to ask, but what happened after I left?" He noted his grandmother had lost weight and her clothes while clean, were torn and tattered. She always prided herself on looking her best.

"Ye saw the worst of it, Braeden. The only one's left were the few who managed to escape. They killed everyone else. 'Tis been a long cold winter that's nae done yet, many have died. Frozen because they had no where to go and only the clothes on their back."

Braeden was saddened to hear it. He knew it wouldnae be good news he'd hear, but he had hoped that some miracle perhaps had occurred to save them after he'd departed. He'd only been gone a short time, but somehow time in 1692 had moved more quickly and his Grannie had endured much hardship during the winter months since he'd been gone.

"I'm so sorry," Tessa said as she rose to console Braeden. "I'm thankful that you managed to escape."

"I should have stayed and fought." Braeden finally allowed himself to feel all the overwhelming fear, sadness and confusion he'd been bottling up since that fateful day. His shoulders slumped and he hung his head, feeling shamed that he'd run away.

Standing behind him, Tessa wrapped her arms around him, giving him the love and support he needed so very much in that moment.

"Ye would've been killed, son. There was no point to that. I watched as the Campbell's came towards you and I saw you melt away before their eyes." Grannie was busily cutting up some cheese and bread, pouring ale into wooden cups for them to drink and placing what appeared to be scones on the plate. "I would've laughed if it had occurred at any other time. I believe they were quite addled by it, as they all ran screaming from the sight."

"You were nearby then?" Braeden lifted his head and perked up at this news. "Aye. I had hidden behind some brush amidst the trees. They didnae see me and they were gone so quickly, it was as if they too had disappeared. I was happy you managed to get away. Your father wanted you to go to the meadows. He told me it was important."

"Braeden, do you know what Niall was talking about when we left? He said something about seeing your mother." Tessa moved to his side and gazed up at him.

"My mother is dead, isnae that true Grannie?"

"I thought 'twas. She had gone with yer Da to this place called the meadows. They left you with me, fearing that the travel would be too dangerous. I thought they'd return for ye as soon as they could, but I didnae see my daughter again." Sadness tinged Esther's voice. "Yer Da returned about twelve years later without her. She was my only girl, ye ken. Yer Da was quite ill when he returned. He didnae wish for ye to see him that way. He was talking gibberish most of the time. He gave me the watch with instructions to give it to ye when the massacre occurred. I didnae ken his meaning. He couldn't explain, he was so close to death and he faded in and out. He said ye should wish to see yer mother, or possibly he wished ye could see yer mother. I wasnae too sure. His voice was low and barely audible. I asked him if she was dead, and I thought he said yes, but then he took a violent fit of coughing and when he was able to speak again, his last words to me were for ye to wish to go to the meadows. He no sooner got the words out than he passed." Esther was close to tears now and Braeden went to her, enfolding her in his arms. This woman who had loved and cared for him all his life had suffered greatly. He only hoped he could make it up to her.

"So 'tis possible my mother is still alive and in Las Vegas?" The words escaped his lips on a hopeful whisper.

"Las Vegas?" Esther dried her eyes and tipped her head in question.

"The meadows, Grannie," Braeden answered. "I didnae see her. How was I to find her? I didnae even ken she could be there."

"Braeden, calm yerself. I'm sorry if I didnae make it clear to ye, but 'twas nae clear to me. I didnae ken if my Iona be alive or dead. I didnae wish to get yer hopes up that she was. It all seemed so unbelievable to me. The time travel, the watch. I had nae idea it would even work. Yer Da was out of his mind with sickness when he spoke with me. I thought mayhap he were seeing and hearing things that were nae true."

Braeden sank down on his haunches, head in hands. "I've got to go back for her. If Niall Campbell has her, who knows what he'll do to her."

Tessa knelt on the floor next to Braeden. "We'll go back as soon as we can. We'll find her. Don't worry."

"Aye. We must go back, but I'm afraid if we do, Niall will be waiting for us and we may all end up dead at his hands." Braeden stood and paced back and forth in the tiny room. Two steps one way and two steps the other.

"I'm not so worried about his hands. It's his magick that we should fear," Bobby said. "Esther, allow me." He took the plates of food from Braeden's grandmother and set them on the table.

"I'm sorry. 'Tis all I have to offer ye." They all took their seats and waited for Esther to join them before digging in.

"A good plan is what ye need." Grannie passed the plates of food around. "Nothing important was ever accomplished without one."

"We're going back, but you're coming with us, Esther." Tessa was about to take a tentative bite of the tiny scone that Esther had set before her.

"Ye'll be needing some fresh butter and honey for that. I dinnae have much, but I'll share the last of my larder with ye." She handed them to Tessa, who slathered the scone with both. "I dinnae think this time travel is fer me. I'll stay here in me own home."

"Mmm... that's the most delicious scone I've ever had." Tessa's eyes were alight as she licked the honey from her lips.

"Grannie is the best baker in all of Scotland," Braeden proudly stated.

"I dinnae ken the rest of Scotland but at least in Glencoe, Braeden."

"We need someone at The Albannach who can bake scones like these," Tessa said. "We'd love to have you, Esther."

"We've more important things to discuss. As I've said, we must come up with a plan." Esther obviously didn't wish to talk about it.

"We can go back the same way we came. I would hope that we wouldnae end up at The Magick Society, but at The Albannach." Braeden stated between the final sips of ale that Esther had just pored for them.

"The Albannach, what is this ye speak of?"

"It's my father's casino and resort," Tessa answered.

Esther nodded. She appeared resigned to the confusion of all this talk. "You'll see it when we get back," Bobby said.

"Oh, I don't believe I can go anywhere with you." Esther vigorously shook her head.

"Why nae, Gran. There's nae a thing to keep you here anymore, yer almost out of food and there's still much winter to come." Braeden caught her hand in his and held it before she could move away.

She seemed to give this some thought and as she spoke, and Braeden couldn't help but note how weak and frail she appeared. "I've lived here all my life and I thought I'd die here as well. My dear friends have all gone on to meet their maker and yet I'm still here. I've wondered why. Why is it that I've been spared? I was lucky to have enough food to get me to this point, but truthfully when I baked this last batch of scones, even though my supplies had dwindled to almost nothing, I wanted to taste them once more before it was my turn to pass. Mayhap yer returning now, as ye did, is a sign. A sign that 'tis nae time fer me to leave this life." She silently gazed at her small cottage and then with a renewed strength, said, "Yer most probably right. I am alone here and I have always loved a good adventure. I'll go."

"Ye'll see some most unusual things, but ye mustnae fear. In time it will all seem normal to ye," Braeden explained.

Esther laughed heartily and the others glanced back and forth to each other in question. "I wonder where it is ye'll be taking me. I hadn't thought to ask before this. I know 'tis the meadows, but I know nothing else."

"Las Vegas in the year 2016. The future." Braeden took hold of her hand as she sucked in a deep breath and gasped at this new information.

"The future. My, my. I wouldnae believe it possible if ye werenae sitting here before me in yer strange clothing and speaking strangely as well." She spoke directly to Tessa and Bobby.

"Do you think you'd like to go?" Bobby asked. It was obvious he'd felt an immediate bond with Esther, which made Braeden smile. Going to Las Vegas with them would be a huge change for his grandmother, but on the other hand it might be another chance for her to live a long and happy life. After all, she'd have food, shelter and her family to take care of her. That would hardly be possible here in this time. She had no one and chances of her meeting a man like Bobby were practically nonexistent.

"Aye. I'd like to go. I'd like it verra much. But I'm an old woman. I'm nae sure I could survive the journey." Esther smiled sweetly at them all.

"Esther. You are not old. I won't hear it." Bobby objected. "In Las Vegas you'd be considered closer to middle aged, with many years ahead of you to live a happy and fulfilling life." His eyes sparkled when he spoke to Esther and she blushed at his words.

Esther thought about this momentarily and then taking a big breath and releasing it, said, "Well, as long as ye'll all be there with me I think I'd be most happy there. And Bobby, ye'd make sure I got there safely?"

"Of course, Esther. I wouldn't allow anything to happen to you." Bobby had come to life since they'd been here. Braeden had seen the beginnings of it when Bobby spelled the watch in Niall's drawing room and with each passing minute he seemed to be changing into a much more confident sorcerer.

Bobby continued gazing at Esther as she spoke. "Good. One part of the plan solved. Now we need to discuss Niall Campbell and your mother."

They talked for many hours and long after it was dark. "My father's going to be worried about us." Tessa hadn't thought about him until just this moment. "We've got to get back quickly. I don't want him going to Niall looking for us." She had a moment of panic, looking to Braeden and Bobby. "What if Niall tries to harm him? He's probably pretty angry that he's lost the watch."

"Aye. 'Twill do us nae good to think on that now. We need some rest. Traveling through time takes a lot out of a person. We should sleep here tonight and in the morning we'll head back. Bobby, do ye believe ye can make the watch work again?"

"Before we are ready to leave, I'll charm the hands once again so that they move all the way around the clock face as they did before."

Relief spread across Braeden's face. "We'll sleep then."

There wasn't much room in the tiny one-room cottage that Esther called home, but they made the best of it. Esther offered her bed to Tessa, who refused on the grounds that she'd been camping many times and didn't mind sleeping on the floor.

They laid out blankets across the floor and close to the fire. Esther climbed into bed and the other three lay down on the hard floor and made themselves as comfortable as possible. Once Braeden was in his spot, he pulled Tessa into his arms and cradled her to him. She rested her head on his chest and before long was asleep. He could hear Bobby softly snoring and his grandmother's even breathing. He closed his eyes, knowing that tomorrow could go well or it could go horribly wrong. They had no way of knowing.

BRIGHT AND EARLY the next morning, they gathered in a clearing near the house Esther had called home for many, many years.

"I believe that the key is that we all hold onto each other," Braeden stated.

They gathered in a circle and hugged each other tightly. Braeden used his free arm to hold the watch to his chest and he wished with all his heart for them to return to Las Vegas and to John McTavish.

It didn't happen as quickly this time and he wondered if it had something to do with the extra person going with them. Nevertheless, he continued wishing and he encouraged the others to do the same. They all began muttering the same thing. "We wish to return to Las Vegas and to John McTavish."

Braeden hoped that by mentioning John's name they would end up at The Albannach instead of with Niall Campbell. He closed his eyes and felt the world around him spinning and a great wind blowing. He felt the others tighten their grip on him and after only moments, he opened his eyes to find the four of them strewn across John McTavish's office.

"What the...?" John jumped up from his desk and ran to them. "Where did you come from? I've been searching all over for you. I called Detective Nance and he'll be on his way over shortly."

"It's okay, Da. You can call Detective Nance and tell him there's no need for him to come. We're alright and we've brought Braeden's Gran back with us."

"I see you have. Bobby's with you as well. What happened?" The worried expression on John's face hadn't been alleviated by their appearance.

"We had to travel back in time to escape Niall." Braeden explained what had taken place at the Las Vegas Society for Magick and Sorcery and how the only way to escape was to go back in time. "I'm sorry to trouble ye, but we had no choice."

"I'm just happy you're all okay. And please excuse my poor manners Mrs. MacDonald. I'm quite pleased to make your acquaintance." John held out a hand to help her up from the rug.

Esther had a look of awe on her face as she gaped at John and at everything else she was seeing. "I'm pleased to meet you as well, sir."

"Please, call me John. I keep telling Braeden that same thing, but he always reverts to sir." John glanced in Braeden's direction with a cocked eyebrow and stern expression.

They all rose to their feet. Braeden was happy they'd all made it back in one piece. This time travel was all new to him and he had no idea how it worked or why it worked. He was just thrilled that he'd been able to transport everyone and get them here safely. His greatest fear was that someone would be lost on the way and end up in another time and place where he wouldn't be able to find them. That hadn't happened and he breathed a sigh of relief.

"I'm happy we're back, but I have to admit I would've liked to explore your time more before we left," Tessa said.

"I agree," Bobby chimed in. "The little bit we saw was fascinating. I've always been a history buff and I can't think of anything better than actually being able to see history in the making."

"We have bigger problems at the moment," Braeden reminded them.

"Yes. It seems we do." John agreed.

"From what I've learned and what Niall said before we escaped, he knows where my mother is. He may even be holding her hostage to get the watch."

"We have to find her and we have to stop Niall. He plans to use the watch to rob The Albannach and some other casinos, ruin you Da and then travel to a future time and place where he can live in luxury." Tessa stood by Braeden's side, holding his arm.

"I thought as much. I was fairly sure he was behind the incident with the safe and I'm sure Margaret Camden is somehow involved as well," John said.

"She is. I saw her leaving The Society before I went in. She has to be in league with Niall," Braeden stated.

"We can't let him get his hands on the watch. After rescuing Braeden's mother, that's the most important thing." Tessa said.

"Agreed. Let's figure this out. I put a call in to Niall earlier to see if he knew where you were. He hasn't returned it yet, but maybe he will if he knows you're here with the watch."

"That would surely get his attention," Braeden said.

"Well, let's get our ducks in a row then before I call him again. We need to have a clear plan and we need to somehow overcome his magick."

"I can do that," Bobby said. "He got the better of me last time because I wasn't prepared for his attack. This time I'm going to beat him at his own game."

"Niall's a pretty powerful sorcerer, how are you going to do that?" Tessa questioned.

"Bobby's equally as powerful, Tessa. He just chose not to use his powers to aid Niall and Niall has never forgiven him for that," John explained.

"All true. If I can ensnare him in a magick web, we can send him off to that future time and place without benefit of all the money he wants. Braeden, that means you'll need to go with him to get him there and then you'll need to use the watch to get back here again."

"Aye. I can do that." Braeden felt confident that with Bobby's help, he could do this.

"No." Tessa sounded anxious. "No. I don't want you to do that, Braeden. It's too dangerous."

"I'll be fine, lass. I've gotten myself out of many a tough situation and if Bobby does a good job trapping Niall, I should be able to get back before he even has a chance to undo the spell."

"He's right," Bobby said. "I can make the spell last for a certain amount of time and that would allow Braeden to get back."

"But how will he get back. You've had to spell the watch both times we've used it, and you'll have to do it again so he can take Niall away. If you're not there to spell the watch, how will he get back?" Tessa didn't appear too comfortable with this whole plan, and she wasn't agreeing to anything until she knew Braeden would be returning to her when it was over.

"I guess I'll just have to go with him then. With the two of us there, I've no doubt that everything will go according to plan." Bobby glanced up at Braeden, who nodded in approval.

"Now, to get your mother back." John brought them all back to the most important aspect of their plan. The safe return of Iona.

CHAPTER *20*

*I*T WAS IMPERATIVE that they convince Niall to bring Iona to John's office where he believed he would exchange her for the watch. Once they had them both there, if all went according to plan, Bobby would be hiding nearby and he'd weave his spell and disable Niall's ability to conjure any magick from that moment until he was removed and sent to a future time and place.

Tessa would have liked to see him pay for murdering Danny and Kenneth, but she realized that Niall alive and in Las Vegas at this time was a very bad idea. They could have him arrested, but with his magick, who knew what he would do to free himself. They'd poured over maps and discussed at length where they would send Niall so that he could do the least amount of damage, and had finally settled on a remote atoll in the Pacific Ocean just one year in the future. There would be no need to send him further forward in time, as he wouldn't be able to harm any of them from his new home. It would be difficult for him to harm *anyone* from there. Tessa was worried, but she had faith in Bobby and Braeden. She paced back and forth in the lobby of her father's office. He'd made the phone call about an hour ago, but hadn't heard anything since. What was taking so long?

"Sit, Tessa. Yer pacing isn't going to make him arrive any sooner." Braeden caught her hand as she passed and pulled her down next to him on the sofa.

Kelly had been sent home. They didn't want to risk any harm coming to her. They'd told her of their plan on the off chance that if something went wrong, she could relay the information to the police. She, of course, had been shocked by all the information she received, but promised she'd help in any way she could.

John finally came out of his office, a serious look on his face. "He finally called me back. He'll be here soon and he's bringing your mother with him. Bobby, you'll need to get yourself in position in the hidden room behind my office walls. Can you pull this off from back there."

"I can. The wall won't get in my way." He seemed very confident and that put everyone a little more at ease. Braeden's Grannie was back in their private apartments, out of harm's way. Kelly would take care of her if anything happened to them. John led Bobby through his office and into the secret room behind his desk. There was nothing left to do now but wait. And wait they did. An hour went by and then another. Whatever Niall was up to, it couldn't be good. Was he going to beat them at their own game, or was there some other reason for his delay?

Finally, the elevators to John's office floor opened and they all waited nervously for Niall to walk the length of the hall and enter through the foyer doors. A beautiful woman was at his side, dressed in jeans, a t-shirt and a cropped jacket. She was wearing the prettiest red high heels Tessa had ever seen. If this was Braeden's mother, she looked anything but motherly. She was stunning. Tessa glanced in Braeden's direction as he stood staring at the woman. They'd discussed it and he had no memory of her at all as she'd left while he was still quite little, so this was certainly a shock to him.

The woman quickly glanced in his direction and almost fell. Niall grabbed her arm and steadied her. "Yes. That's him." He confirmed. "Yer son in the flesh."

She broke free of Niall and went to Braeden, standing in front of him. Seemingly mesmerized, she reached out a hand and touched his cheek, stroking it lovingly. A lone tear trailed down her cheek. "Braeden. Is it really ye?"

Braeden seemed unable to speak and everyone present was enthralled by this moment. Finally he grasped her hand in his and brought it to his mouth, where he placed a reverent kiss on it. "Mother. 'Tis me."

"You look just like your father. So handsome." As she was about to hug Braeden, Niall grabbed her arm and pulled her away. She nearly fell again, but he steadied her.

"We can't have ye getting hurt. After all, ye are my key to that watch and as such, ye will not leave my side until I tell ye that you can go. Do ye understand me?"

"Aye." Tears sprung to her eyes and she hung her head in what Tessa saw as an attempt to hide them from her son, but Braeden was already bristling at this treatment of his mother and was about to leap across the room at Niall when Tessa put a calming hand on his arm.

"Good. Now, John, I've done as ye asked. I brought Braeden's mother. Where's my watch?" Niall impatiently tapped his foot on the carpet.

"It's in my office. Please come in and I'll get it for ye." John led the way and the others followed.

"Ye'd better not be up to something. It won't end well for ye if ye are."

"I wouldn't worry about that. Ye'll be getting what ye want in short order," John assured him.

They entered the room, John heading to his desk, Niall and Iona to the center of the room. The others stood on the outer edges of the room with the exception of Braeden who stood near to Niall, but far enough away that he couldn't get his hands on the watch.

"The watch. Now." Niall put out his hand for the it. He was growing impatient.

As they'd rehearsed prior to Niall's arrival, John said, "Braeden, would you hand Niall the watch please."

As Braeden reached into his sporran for the watch, they heard a commotion outside of the office. Niall grabbed Iona by the arm as they all turned to see Margaret Camden running towards the office, and on her heels was Detective Nance.

Things moved quickly from this point. Bobby was unaware of what was happening, and so he continued crafting his spell. Margaret threw herself at Niall and held on for dear life, dislodging Iona in the process. Tessa grabbed Iona by the arm and moved her away from Niall, who was caught off guard when the wall opened and a tornado whisked into the room, spinning around him. Niall and Margaret were caught in the wind that was slowing tying them together into a human knot. Niall was unable to extricate his arms or hands to fire back at Bobby, and Detective Nance's eyes appeared as if they might pop right out of his head as he stood stock still, unable to move. Bobby exited the room, his appearance now one of a great sorcerer. He'd always seemed meek and mild to the others, but the man they saw now had fire in his eyes and seemed to have grown a foot taller. His incantation rang through the room as he pointed his wand at Niall, who was frozen, unable to defend against this onslaught. Finally the wind died down and, though John's office was a mess of papers, everyone was smiling with relief.

"What just happened?" Detective Nance had recovered from his initial shock. "And who was that woman. She saw me coming into the casino and she ran to the elevators. I followed her because she seemed somewhat distressed. She cringed in the corner of the elevator all the way up. I tried talking to her, but she wouldn't or couldn't speak and when the doors opened she bolted out. I wasn't sure what she was doing, so I ran after her."

"That's Margaret Camden," John told him.

"The lady with the safe?" Detective Nance asked.

"Yes. She's the one." John turned away from Detective Nance toward Braeden. "Braeden, it's up to you now."

Braeden held the watch close to his heart. "I'm going with him," Tessa said.

"Nae. I cannae chance losing you. Bobby and I will be back as quickly as we can."

'Where are they going?" Detective Nance asked.

Niall appeared panic stricken as he opened his mouth to cry out, but nothing came forth. Braeden, followed by Bobby went to him and placing his hand on Niall's shoulder, while Bobby did the same, he wished to go to the future, far away from Las Vegas, to that small atoll in the Pacific as they'd agreed upon. He muttered the latitude and longitude over and over, along with the date of February 2017. He watched the faces of the others as his wish became reality. One minute they were there and the next gone. And Braeden, Bobby, Niall and Margaret travelled through time and space until they landed on a remote island where Niall would have a hard time doing any harm to anyone ever again.

Braeden wasted no time doing as Bobby had instructed. He deposited Niall on the sandy shore of this island beach and moved far away from him. Now it was Bobby's turn. Before he recited the incantation that would free Niall and Margaret, he recharged the watch, moving the hands around the dial so they could escape when they were finished in this place.

"Margaret, can you hear me?" Bobby asked.

"Yes." Her voice was shaky and they could see she was shocked by what had just occurred.

"Do you wish to stay here with Niall? We can bring ye back to Las Vegas, if ye dinnae." Braeden didn't want to leave her here if that wasn't what she wanted.

"No. I'll stay with Niall. I love him. Besides, I can't go back. I'll be arrested for tampering with the safe. When I saw Niall heading to the elevators up to John's office I knew I had to follow him. That's when I saw that cop. I thought he was there for me and I panicked. I don't want to go back. I can't go to jail. Please leave me here with my Niall."

Bobby spelled the watch and then recited his incantation. Niall and Margaret were slowly unraveled from their magical prison. Braeden and Bobby took this opportunity to wish on the watch again. He wished to be back in Las Vegas with Tessa. Nothing happened.

"We've got to get out of here. He'll be free in a matter of minutes." Bobby shouted. "Try again."

Braeden did as Bobby instructed, this time taking a moment to focus and relax. "Hurry," Bobby cried. "He's almost free."

With the watch close to his heart and one arm around Bobby, Braeden wished again. "I wish to go back to Las Vegas, to Tessa McTavish, to the year 2016 from whence we came." He wasn't sure it had worked, but then just as the last bit of web was unraveled, freeing Niall and Margaret, he felt it. They were being sucked back through time. Niall angrily ran towards them, but Margaret stopped him and they both watched until Braeden could no longer see them.

"WHERE HAVE YOU been? What took so long?" Tessa ran to him, touching his arms and chest to make sure he was real. Satisfied that he was, she stood back waiting for a response.

"Have we been gone that long? It seemed only moments."

"You've been gone hours son," John said.

"Hopefully, we've seen the last of Niall Campbell." Bobby seemed energized and completely new. No longer the sad and down-trodden man he'd been only days ago. "Now, if you'll excuse me, I'm heading over to The Society to get my rightful spot back as the CES."

"CES?" Tessa asked.

"Yes, the Chief Executive Sorcerer. The others should be happy to have me back. They all feared Niall and will be relieved he's gone."

"Bobby should have been the CES before Niall stole the position," John explained.

Braeden listened carefully, but really only had one thing on his mind. He went to his mother. "Mother, I thought ye were dead."

She took his hands in hers and gazed lovingly at him. "My son. I've longed for this moment for so many years. I'm sorry I wasn't there for you when you were growing up. I'm sorry I left you, but I never expected to be gone for such a long time." Tears welled in her eyes and she rested her head on his chest. Braeden took her in his arms and consoled her as best he could. Any anger or abandonment he felt when he first learned she was alive and in Las Vegas evaporated into nothing. He understood his mother loved him and that it had been equally difficult for her. Perhaps even more so.

"We've much to talk about. Grannie is here, too. She can't wait to see you."

"I called Kelly to come back in after you left. I've sent her to get Esther," John offered.

The words had no sooner left his mouth when Esther came through the doors, scanning the faces in the room until she found her daughter. "Iona, I've missed ye so." She began to cry and could hardly contain herself. Both Braeden and his mother went to her.

Braeden guided her to a chair, taking her hands. "Grannie, all is well. Ye'll not be parted from either of us ever again."

Iona hugged her mother. "I'm so sorry I couldnae get back to ye. Thank ye for caring for Braeden. He grew to be the man I'd have wanted him to be and 'tis because of ye."

Braeden took both women in his arms and held onto them tightly. The others in the room, standing silently by, were obviously moved by the reunion of three generations of the MacDonald clan.

"'Tis good to be together again. No matter that it took so many years," Grannie said through happy tears.

"Aye. 'Tis good." Braeden was afraid to move. Afraid they'd disappear on him and he'd be alone.

"So, tell us what happened?" Tessa asked.

"From the beginning?" Iona said. "'Tis a long tale, are ye sure?"

The others all nodded their heads.

"I was a young lass, not more than seventeen when I met Ian Campbell. At first, we were wary of each other, he being a Campbell and I being a MacDonald. There had been much hatred between our clans, but not for us. We would somehow manage to accidentally run into each other at the same time each day, and in the same place."

The other's chuckled at this.

"After nae so much time, we fell deeply in love with each other and wished to be married. Ian spoke with his family and they were appalled at the idea. Mother on the other hand, told me that if we truly loved each other and it was meant to be, then it would be." She cast a loving gaze in her mother's direction. "She was right. We pledged our love to each other. We handfasted, just the two of us. No others were there, and in our hearts we were married. Soon after, I found I was pregnant. Ian and I were still nae living together. Ian hoped that with time he'd be able to convince his clan to accept me, but that was nae to be. The others in our clan wondered who the father of my babe might be and they began asking questions, soon suspecting that Ian may be the one. Braeden was born and shortly after, Ian found that he was the focus of both the MacDonald's and Campbell's anger. We had to escape before we were killed. We wanted to live together with our son in a place where we could live our lives without judgement and fear. Ian had a watch that had been handed down to him from his father. It always went to the first son of the first son. That happened to be Ian and that was also you, Braeden." Iona smiled warmly at Braeden, all the love in her heart shining through. "We werenae sure where the watch would take us, so we decided to go without you, my son. We didnae wish any harm to come to ye, but it was best that yer Da and I leave as soon as possible. I went with him, with the idea in mind that I would come back for ye once I knew it to be safe. It wasn't until after we'd time travelled that we learned that the watch only worked every twelve years."

"How did ye know?" Braeden asked.

"There's an inscription on the back of the watch. It's not plain to see, as 'tis hidden in the scrollwork engraved there."

Braeden turned the watch over in his hand. "Aye. I see it, but 'tis so small and hard to read. I wouldnae ever have know it was there."

Iona took up her story again. "We were both so distraught when we realized that the watch wouldnae work for us again and that you, my son, wouldnae see yer Ma or Da again for many years." Iona paused and Tessa gave her a glass of water, which she gladly drank. "Unfortunately, at that time we met Niall Campbell and it was his wanting of the watch that made it impossible for me to return to ye." She nodded to her mother and Braeden. "He'd been our friend since we arrived. He'd helped us, given us a place to live and took care of us for twelve years, all the while trying to convince Ian to give him the watch. Finally, when he knew the watch would work again, he told Ian he wanted it. He planned to use it to rob the casinos and to then escape." She shook her head at that. "Ian wouldnae allow him to have it, so he used his magic to lock me away in his basement. Yer father would come and speak with me every day. Out of curiosity we had been reading history books about Scotland and so we knew there was to be a massacre at Glencoe in 1692. That was in twelve years time. We had to get the watch back to ye, Braeden, so yer father and I agreed that he would go back and give you the watch. He planned to return with ye, but I dinnae see him here." Her eyes searched the faces in the room. "What happened to my Ian? Where is he?" Iona looked to her mother for answers and it was with great sadness that Esther relayed what had occurred. Tears shone in Iona's eyes. "I hoped and prayed that he would return to me with you, Braeden, but deep in my heart I knew he wouldnae make the return trip." She took a moment to collect her thoughts and wipe her eyes with the tissue Tessa handed her.

When she was ready, she continued. "As for Niall, he held me captive for all those many years. No longer in the cell, he kept me bound where I was through magic. I couldnae leave the grounds of the Society, unless I was escorted. He never treated me poorly, but he wouldnae allow me my freedom either. He wanted that watch so very badly and was determined to have it, no matter how long it might take. Yer Da tried to explain to him that he'd nae be able to use it because he wasn't from the right Campbell line, but he wouldnae hear it. He said his magick was powerful enough to overcome that obstacle."

"Yer Ian was far too ill to return to ye, Iona. He loved ye so verra much. Ye were on his mind constantly and while he made little sense during the time he was back, yer name was always on his lips. He gave me the watch and told me to have Braeden wish to go to the meadows. I didnae understand what he meant, but I repeated it to myself every day, lest I forget. Thankfully, I didnae and when the day came that the Campbell's were slaughtering the MacDonald's, I knew I had to give Braeden the watch and send him on his way. I believe ye all ken what happened after that."

Iona wept silently as she listened to the account of her husband's bravery and the illness which led to his death. Being left behind with Niall, she'd had no idea why he hadn't returned for her. She only knew that Niall was very angry about the watch. "Niall was obsessed with it. When Braeden arrived, Niall knew. He said he could feel the watch and that it rightfully should have been passed down to him. He refused to believe that the watch could not be his. Although he was a first son of a first son, it was the wrong clan lines and so he would never have inherited it. No sense could be talked into him. He insisted that the watch would be his. I'm relieved he never got his hands on it, because if Braeden ever has a son of his own, the watch will be his and it will carry on from there, but for now it's at rest here in Las Vegas as strange as that may be."

Tessa was just about to speak, when Iona continued.

"Now you may ask how we came to be in Las Vegas when we time travelled to the future and all I can say is that Ian wished on the watch. He wished to travel to a future time and a future place where we'd be accepted and wanted. Truly Niall Campbell wanted us because we had the watch and that is how we ended up here."

"That's an incredible story and if I hadn't seen you with my own two eyes, I may never have believed it," John said. "I was unaware of you being here, Iona. If I had known, I would have done everything in my power to free you."

Bobby was at Esther's side now, with a comforting hand on her shoulder. "At the time, John and I were friends with Niall. He wasn't an easy man to befriend, but he was a talented sorcerer and as head of The Las Vegas Society for Magick and Sorcery I felt it was my duty to mentor him. It must have been shortly after you arrived with Ian that he started putting his plans in motion, although they would never come to fruition. He began systematically trying to destroy me. At first he'd tried to convince me to dabble in the dark arts, saying there was more money to be made there than from performing in a magick show on The Strip. I refused to even consider it and he became more and more angry. Eventually I'd had enough. He managed to turn all the others against me and I couldn't take another moment of arguing with him, so I left The Society and found myself blacklisted from all the prominent casinos on The Strip. Niall was a powerful sorcerer and he did a good job of hiding you from everyone, I'm sorry to say."

John added, "We waited and waited for Ian's return, but it never happened. So when you walked into my office that first day, I knew exactly who you were, Braeden. For one thing, you are the spitting image of your father and for another, you seemed as if you'd just arrived from another time. I'd been expecting you for many, many years and then you finally arrived and I'm so happy that you did. Even though I've seen it with my own eyes, it's still a surprise to me that time travel is really possible."

Everyone chuckled at this and then Bobby spoke up. "Where did Detective Nance go? He must have been shocked to see us disappear like that."

"He sure was," Tessa answered. "We explained everything to him. He listened carefully to us, before turning around and walking out."

"I'm sure he needs to process everything he saw and then come up with something to tell his superiors that won't make him look like he's lost his mind." John gazed around the room at everyone. "So, now that we've all told our stories, if we can stay put for a while, I think we need to celebrate this happy day. Your family has been reunited, Braeden and we've banished Niall Campbell to some future hell of his own making. I think that calls for a toast."

Kelly arrived accompanied by one of the resort sommeliers with bottles of chilled champagne and flutes for everyone. They lifted their glasses and toasted to their good fortune.

"John, I have something I'd like to ask ye." Braeden got very serious. "Of course, Braeden, ask away."

"Sir, I'd like your permission to marry yer daughter."

Tessa gasped and covered her mouth with her hands. Everyone's eyes turned to her. "Braeden, you haven't even asked me," Tessa blurted out.

Braeden wasn't sure which way to turn. He was still waiting for his answer from John, but now he wasn't so sure he'd need his permission. Would Tessa marry him? He was caught between father and daughter, sure he'd just made some horrible mistake, which would end in disaster for the future he hoped to share with Tessa.

"Tessa, in Braeden's time it was the way things were done. Besides, I'm giving him permission. Now it's up to you to decide if you'd like to marry him."

Braeden looked hopefully in her direction. She wasn't saying anything and he wasn't sure why. His stomach was all in knots, but he kept his expression neutral. When she still didn't answer, he realized what he was supposed to do and he went to her. "Tessa, I never thought that I could fall in love with someone as quickly as I have with ye. From the moment I laid eyes on ye, my angel, I knew ye were the one fer me. It would be an honor to be yer husband. Tessa, will ye marry me?"

She didn't make him wait this time. "Yes, Braeden. I will marry you. I love you and I want to be your wife."

"I have no fancy engagement ring to give ye, but I am giving ye me heart. 'Tis yers to keep now and fer always." Braeden took her in his arms and kissed her, the woman he loved and was meant to be with. He was happier than he'd ever been.

TESSA COULDN'T BELIEVE she was going to marry this man she loved so very much. "Congratulations to ye, Tessa. Ye'll be me daughter. I'm so happy." Iona kissed her cheek and held her hand.

"And ye'll be me granddaughter," Esther added, hugging her tightly.

Tessa hadn't had the benefit of a mother or grandmother for many years, so she was ecstatic knowing she now had these two sweet women in her life. To this point it was just Tessa and her father. She'd always wanted to be part of a large family and now she was. The private family compound would be a little more crowded from now on, but that didn't matter. They'd all be together.

CHAPTER 21

THINGS COULDN'T BE more perfect in Tessa's world. Although she wasn't married yet, she and Braeden were now sharing a room, while Iona and Esther took the other upstairs bedroom. Her father was in the process of building another cottage for Tessa and Braeden in the private compound. There would be plenty of room for a cozy little place where they could be alone and enjoy each other's company. They would also be getting their own private pool. Naughty thoughts ran through her head as she remembered the first time Braeden made love to her by the pool, and then *in* the pool.

Tessa's phone rang, interrupting her thoughts. She took a moment to compose herself before answering.

"Hello?"

"Hi, Tessa. It's me, Kelly. Your father wanted to know if he could expect to see you in your office today or if you were taking the day off." The playful sound of Kelly's voice told Tessa that her father was teasing her.

"Tell him I'll be there soon. Braeden's already working and I'm just checking in on the progress at our new place." She took one final look at the little cottage.

"How's it coming along?" Kelly asked.

"Good. It should be done by the time we get back from our honeymoon." Tessa walked back towards the main house as they spoke.

"I'll bet you can't wait."

"That's putting it mildly. I wish I could use Braeden's watch to take us to the future date of our wedding. I just want to be married, Kelly. I don't care about all this other stuff." And she really didn't. She'd get married at one of those quickie-wedding chapels on The Strip if it wouldn't be a major disappointment to her father.

"Sure you do. Besides, it's not just for you. It's for Braeden, his mother and grandmother, your father. And, you'd probably be sorry later if you didn't go all out for this. Hopefully, you're only going to get married once, right?"

"I'm definitely only getting married once, Kelly. Braeden and I are perfect for each other. There could never be anyone else for me." Tessa couldn't believe Kelly would even suggest that.

"I'm sorry, Tess. I didn't mean it like that." Kelly sounded contrite to Tessa's ears.

"When are you and Sean getting married?" She felt the need to change the topic, so she wouldn't have to answer any more questions.

"He hasn't asked me. You know that." Kelly sounded disappointed and Tessa felt bad that she'd put her on the spot like that.

"He will. He loves you. It's plain to see for anyone with eyes."

"And I love him. I'm just not sure he's the marrying kind."

"Time will tell, Kelly. Just enjoy what you've got for now." She reached the house and headed inside to change her clothes. "I better get going. Tell my father I'll be therein no time."

"Okay. See you soon."

Setting her phone down, Tessa grabbed some clothes from her closet and changed from her yoga pants and top to a pencil skirt and a white blouse. She fixed her hair and makeup and headed off to work, thinking about how lucky she was.

THE DAY OF the wedding had finally arrived and early that morning, Tessa took Esther and Iona to the spa for massages, manicures and makeovers.

Esther in particular was very impressed with the pampering she received. "Tessa, I can't believe after all those many years of life in Scotland's past, where I worked harder than many a man and never took a moment to pamper myself, here I am being treated like a queen!"

Hearing Esther's words put a satisfied smile on Tessa's face. "You deserve to be treated like a queen, Esther. You've worked hard your whole life and now is the time for you to reap the rewards."

Esther laughed heartily, clasping Tessa's hands. "You me dear, are a gem of a lass. Braeden is lucky to have found ye. And what about ye, Iona? What do ye think of all of this?" Esther asked.

"'Tis always a pleasure to do something like this." she responded.

"Ye sound as if this is nae yer first time." Esther tipped her head in wonder. "Although Niall could be as mean as a hornet at times, he saw to it that even as his prisoner I was treated well. I know that 'twas

Margaret Camden who convinced him that I needed a wardrobe, shoes, and other womanly things. She would accompany me on outings. We'd shop, go to the beauty salon, have lunch. She didn't have many friends and she treated me kindly. It made my time in Niall's custody bearable. I don't know how I would have fared if she hadnae been there. Niall seemed happy to make Margaret happy and if my being her friend made her happy, then he would allow it… for her."

"Why didn't you try to escape or tell someone you met about your situation?" Tessa wondered.

"I was still under lock and key. Niall put a spell on me that kept me from running away. I was physically unable to be more than ten feet away from Margaret at any time when we were out.

I never told anyone because he convinced me that they would never believe me and they'd think me not right in the head. I'd be locked away somewhere in far worse conditions than I already had and I wouldnae be allowed to leave. I was too scairt to do anything but obey his commands."

Tessa retreated into her own thoughts, wondering about Niall and Margaret. How were they faring on their little island in the middle of nowhere? No doubt Niall had used his sorcery to create everything they needed in the way of food and shelter. His exile had been the best possible solution to an intricate problem. At least he couldn't harm anyone else with his magic and more importantly, he was far away from Las Vegas, with no way of getting back. Detective Nance had been by a few times to speak with her father. John dropped the charges against Margaret, so that solved part of his problem, but after realizing that he had no way at all to explain what he'd learned to his superiors, Detective Nance managed to find a way to convince them that with the lack of evidence to show Danny and Kenneth had been murdered, the case wouldn't be solved any time soon.

John and Tessa set up a trust fund for Kenneth's children and they bought his wife a townhouse in a much better part of town. Mrs. Carra was told they would always be a part of The Albannach family and could come to John at any time if they ever needed anything. She told him she needed to work and he saw to it that she was hired in the human resources department.

"Oh, my! Look at me. Do ye think Bobby will recognize me, Tessa?" Esther was beaming at her reflection in the mirror.

Tessa shook herself back to the present and was pleased that her mother-in-law and grandmother-in-law looked amazing. She chuckled to herself at Esther's question.

Esther and Bobby had become quite an item since they'd been back.

He was back in his position of CES at the Society and had made it a priority to woo Esther every chance he got. He took her out to fancy restaurants, bought her lovely little gifts just to let her know how much she meant to him and he was happy to show her off to everyone he knew here in Vegas. "I wouldn't worry about that, Esther. He'll love it."

"I hope so, because I do. Thank ye so much, dear."

"Yes. Thank you, Tessa. You've been so wonderful to us both." Iona smiled warmly at her daughter-in-law to be.

"You're welcome. I'm happy to do it. I love you both. Without you there'd be no Braeden for me to love." She hugged each one in turn, kissing them on the cheek. "Now, let's go get dressed."

BRAEDEN STOOD FIDGETING at the altar of The Albannach wedding chapel. To his eyes it was simply beautiful and a testament to his wife's talent for planning and ultimately creating a memorable event. He couldn't imagine what was taking so long. He felt he'd already been standing there for hours, when the sound of the bagpipes playing *The Mist Covered Mountains of Home*, a song Tessa had chosen especially for him, floated through the chapel. A smile lit his lips as he saw his beautiful bride being escorted down the aisle by John McTavish. Everyone stood and watched as the two passed by on their way to meet Braeden. He noted that his mother and grandmother had their hankies out as tears of happiness tumbled down their cheeks.

All of Braeden's nervousness vanished the moment John placed Tessa's hand in his. She was his beautiful angel and had been from the day he'd first met her. Now he was going to spend the rest of his life loving her and he was impatient to get started.

"THE CEREMONY WAS so beautiful, Tessa!" As the maid of honor, Kelly was busy fixing Tessa's train for more photos.

"You know I arranged the whole thing, but I hardly took the time to notice any of it. All I could see from the moment I walked through the chapel doors was my handsome husband." She took a moment to reflect on those words. "I can't believe it. He's my husband. It sounds so strange coming from my mouth, but so right."

"Did I hear ye mentioning me, wife?" Braeden appeared at her shoulder, chuckling at what he'd obviously just overheard.

"Yes, husband. I was just telling Kelly how handsome you looked standing at the altar."

The photographer positioned the two of them and gave them direction on posing as she snapped away.

"I dinnae understand how this works," Braeden pointed to the camera.

"It's a camera. Instead of posing for someone back in your time who would paint a portrait, the camera can take hundreds of portraits of us. She's been taking photos all day and when she's done we'll make a wedding album." Tessa kept her voice low so the photographer wouldn't overhear them. She'd have one heck of a time explaining the whole time travel thing.

"I dinnae believe I'll ever stop asking questions, Tessa. I hope ye willnae get tired of answering them." Braeden appeared sincerely worried that she might.

"Never. I'll happily answer all your questions from now until forever." Standing on tiptoe, she kissed his lips just as the photographer rapidly clicked more photos.

"Tessa, we should get the reception started. We don't want you to miss your flight." John McTavish popped his head out of the banquet room and motioned for them to come in.

The reception was small as was the ceremony. Braeden only had his mother and grandmother there, but Tessa had a few more guests on her side. Mostly people she'd known growing up in Las Vegas. Friends from high school and college, people she'd worked with and her father's friends. She was excited to have everyone meet Braeden. He surprised her by being the perfect host. He was very comfortable as they walked around to all the tables and spoke with their guests. She was so proud of him and so proud to call him husband.

Once their meal was finished, the music started and they shared their first dance as a married couple. Tessa had practiced with him so he wouldn't feel lost on the dance floor and he made their first dance a memorable one by sweeping her up into his arms and twirling her around the dance floor. She could hardly contain her giggles as he placed her gently back down.

The others joined them on the dance floor. Everyone was having a wonderful time. Esther and Bobby were dancing. John seeing Iona sitting alone, asked her to accompany him to the dance floor, which she happily did. There was singing, dancing, speech making and then it was time to say good-bye.

"Thank you all for coming," Tessa called as they made their way to the door, confetti raining down all around them.

"Where are you headed for your honeymoon?" Sean asked as he and Kelly accompanied them out.

"We're going to Scotland," Braeden happily announced.

"Your first plane ride. That'll be exciting," Kelly gushed.

When Braeden told Tessa he wanted to honeymoon in Scotland, she wasn't sure it was going to be a good idea. She worried that it might be too sad for him, but he'd reassured her that he would be fine.

"This is my home now. Here with you, but I must see it. See what it has become," Braeden had stated.

She understood his need for closure, so she didn't question it any further. She wanted to see Scotland and had always planned on going someday. Seeing it with Braeden would be a dream come true.

Bobby had graciously conjured up a passport for Braeden and she was keeping her fingers crossed that it would work. Her father arranged, as his wedding gift to them, for a private plane to take them from Las Vegas to Scotland and then back home again.

The only other hurdle to their honeymoon was getting Braeden on that plane. He was suspicious of the silver objects flying over head. They fascinated him, but he couldn't understand how they stayed up there without flapping wings. Tessa took him to the airport several times where they sat and watched the planes take off and land. She hoped it would go a long way to making him more comfortable about flying. She could tell he was still a little nervous, but he was wearing that game face again. She knew him well enough now to know that he didn't want anyone to know that he might be afraid of anything.

BOARDING THE PLANE, Braeden was a little apprehensive. He had no idea what was about to happen and that made him nervous. Tessa had assured him, as had everyone he'd spoken to, that it was a very safe way to travel and it was also the fastest. They'd be in Scotland in a little over twelve hours. An unbelievable feat as far as he was concerned.

The pilot and fight attendant greeted them as they boarded and then left them, giving them their privacy and time to explore the plane as they prepared for take off.

"Just one thing and then you won't see me again. If you need anything at all, press the call button," the flight attendant gave them a knowing smile. "I won't disturb you otherwise." And then she was off to the front of the plane.

"Oh, look!" Tessa exclaimed. "There's a bed. We'll be able to sleep the whole way to Scotland!"

"The bed is good, love, but I dinnae believe ye'll be doing much sleeping." A sexy smile played across his lips as he picked Tessa up and deposited her on the bed.

"Really? What will we be doing?" Tessa ran a slender finger across his lips as she gazed up at him, her sapphire blue eyes bright with desire.

"Why dinnae I just show ye?" He lay down next to her, cradling her body next to his and kissed her with all the passion he was feeling for her. She returned his kiss in equal measure.

"Braeden, I am so, so very happy." To his eyes she was glowing. "Are you so, so very happy, too?"

"Aye, love. I am." And he kissed her again, pouring all the love he felt in his heart into that one kiss and the one after that and the one after that.

Acknowledgments

I'd like to thank my editor, Vicki McGough for her help getting this book ready for publishing. Thank you to my cover artist, Sheri McGathy of Cover Art by Sheri for another beautiful cover. To my friend and author, Gayle Parness and my daughter, Felicia for brainstorming with me when I got stuck. Thank you to the city of Las Vegas for inspiring this story. Thank you to my husband for understanding my preoccupation with getting this book finished. And lastly, but most importantly, thank you to my readers. You've made this journey so very, very enjoyable.

ABOUT THE AUTHOR

Jennae Vale is a best selling author of romance with a touch of magic. As a history buff from an early age, Jennae often found herself daydreaming in history class - wondering what it would be like to live in the places and time periods she was learning about. Writing time travel romance has given her an opportunity to take those daydreams and turn them into stories to share with readers everywhere.

Originally from the Boston area, Jennae now lives in the San Francisco Bay area, where some of her characters also reside. When Jennae isn't writing, she enjoys spending time with her family and her pets, and daydreaming, of course.

Connect with Jennae:

Twitter.com/jealil
Facebook.com/JennaeValeAuthor
www.jennaevaleauthor.com
jennaevaleauthor@gmail.com

www.ingramcontent.com/pod-product-compliance
Lightning Source LLC
Chambersburg PA
CBHW061235170626
46809CB00007B/2684